THE QUIET TYPE

THE DARK HOBBY TRILOGY

SUMMER PRESCOTT

S. PRESCOTT THRILLERS

CHAPTER 1

Susannah Guntzelman was invisible. Not in the traditional sense of the word, of course, but in the far more painful translation where all of humanity simply failed to notice her existence. She'd been overlooked and unnoticed her entire life, whether at home, by parents who worked too hard to care, or in public, where strangers merely saw a plain, overweight girl, if they saw her at all. Today was no different, as she shuffled to class in last year's jeans and sensible shoes, her mass of dry, frizzy hair carelessly piled atop her head in an unruly bun.

Being invisible had its advantages of course. It allowed her to get through nearly every day of her dreary existence without having to interact with other human beings. Teachers never called on her, no one said hello when they passed her in the hall, and she sat alone during every unending lunch hour, methodically eating the interesting assortment of foods that she'd stuffed into her bright blue insulated lunch pack. The bag was an intrusive spark of color in her otherwise beige existence. She hated it, but her mother, Greta, the long-legged, perfect-haired china doll who loved her job more than her daughter, had said that the store didn't have any black or grey ones, so she would 'just have to deal with it.'

Susannah trailed behind a gaggle of giggling girls, entering the calculus classroom with perhaps less trepidation than the twittering twats in front of her. She was good at math, it came easily to her, and the teacher seemed to know that she might just spiral into a panic attack if she were forced to participate in a way other than quickly scribbling out correct answers and turning them in. Math was orderly. She liked things to be orderly. She was glad, for the teacher's sake, that he somehow understood her need for invisibility.

Early parent/teacher conferences had pegged little Susie as an angry child who didn't get along with others, which led to wretched things. The punishments at home for bad reports were worse than the punishments at school, so she'd learned to keep her seething resentment to herself. She'd kept it to herself for so long, in fact, that she'd grown numb emotionally. Even when battered and taunted mercilessly by thoughtless and cruel classmates, she compressed her mouth into a thin line and kept her head down, waiting until she got home to pick the spit wads from her colorless and tangled hair, and to dab a cold cloth on the welts made by well-aimed rubber bands.

At home, she taught herself to withhold tears from the monster who tried his best to encourage them. When she was stripped naked and whipped with kitchen utensils, belts, shoes, or any other handy device, when she was locked into the chicken coop for days at a time, not even allowed to sleep in her bed or relieve herself in private, and even when she was denied food after the beast who spawned her poked at her soft, white flesh, declaring her to be a fat pig, she'd bite the inside of her cheeks, dig her nails into her palms, or even hold her breath if necessary…but she Would. Not. Cry.

Her goal was simple, wait for the herd of cattle to get out of her way, and get to her seat without bringing any attention to herself. She'd had a rough morning at home, and her nerves were sprinkling dark sparks into her psyche. Susannah was more than ready to immerse herself in the orderly realm of math, glorious math. So focused was she on getting to her seat, that she never saw the furtive foot, encased in an expensive running shoe, darting out like the tongue of a serpent, tripping her.

Arms full of books, the gawky teen hit the ground hard, her head knocking against the metal leg of a desk. There were a few gasps, and more than a few giggles, and when Susannah turned over, stunned, still clutching her books, the concerned frown of Mr. Davis loomed over her.

"Susannah…are you okay? What happened here?" he asked, the cuff of his polyester pants brushing against her arm.

She sat up slowly, dazed, a trickle of defiantly crimson blood running down her forehead, and over the soft round of her cheek. Her heavy glasses were askew, and she pushed them up absently, horrified that every eye in the class was upon her. She flushed bright red from the base of her neck to the roots of her hair, as she heard the guffaws and soft pig sounds of her classmates. Humiliation was an overwhelming emotion that couldn't be stopped, even with years of conditioning. It slammed into her with brute force, threatening to steal the very breath from her lungs. Her head throbbed with it, her mouth turned to cotton, and beads of sweat sprung out on her forehead as she worked to control the tremors which rippled through her. It took her a couple of tries, while the teacher blathered on with his concern and his questions, asking if she needed to go to the nurse, but she rolled herself onto her knees, and leaning on the desk that had struck her, she rose shakily to her feet.

Debbie Moran. Smug, snooty, Debbie Moran was smirking at her, enjoying the result of her sly move. Until this moment, Susannah hadn't loathed her more than any of the other simpering American princesses who glided through the halls as though their nimble feet didn't even touch the chipped linoleum, but now…it was different. Now, dainty little Debbie Moran made something dark rise up inside Susannah the Sow, as her classmates called her, something darker than the judgmental little bitch was prepared to deal with. So dark that it made her heart pound. So dark that it made her mouth water. Soon, Debbie Moran, soon.

Susannah lumbered from the classroom, with Mr. Davis saying something about it being good that she was going to the nurse, but once out of his sight, she bypassed the office and walked out of the school unchallenged, breathing hard, but not from exertion. She huffed and puffed as she walked, striding fast and far as she made her plans, the need for order and justice in her world burning like a hot coal within her.

Teeth clenched, hair blowing in the chill autumn breeze, Susannah swiped absently at the tickle on her cheek, fascinated when she saw blood smeared on her fingers. She turned her hand this way and that, focused on the blood – the rude red color of it. The blood made her think, the blood made her feel, the blood made her hunger. She brought her fingers to her mouth, sucking the crimson liquid in, the metallic blast of it invigorating her. She licked and sucked her fingers until every last trace was gone, and surveyed her pale hand with a slight smile playing about her lips. Soon, Debbie Moran, soon.

Susannah Guntzelman was not a joiner. Participation in school activities was just not something that she did…ever, but when the Student Athletics Association put up a flyer saying that they needed servers for the State Finals Pancake Breakfast, she jumped at the chance. The breakfast was scheduled for mid-November, just before Thanksgiving, so she had just over a month to put her plan into action. She would assimilate…briefly, because it was necessary.

Food was Susannah's solace, and often times her only pleasure. It didn't merely provide her with sustenance, it provided her with an outlet for her sometimes odd creativity. She was usually able to grab a hasty breakfast before her father woke up, although, if she wasn't quite fast enough, he would see her at the table eating, pick up her cereal bowl and dump its contents into the sink. Dinner at the Guntzelman house was a tense affair, where the beast measured every spoonful that was placed on her plate and watched her like a hawk so that she didn't take seconds. But lunch…lunch was Susannah's salvation. She would prepare her noon feast at night, after her father went to bed, and stash it in a cooler in her closet. Experimenting with all sorts of delicious combinations from the refrigerator and pantry, she gorged herself on her creations as she sat in her lonely corner of the lunchroom.

The high school offered cooking classes, and she took every single one, so it seemed quite natural when she volunteered to help out with the athletic club's break-fast, despite her extreme aversion to social situations. She prepared for the event by doing things that she had to do to fit in. Her plan would require some degree of trust from her fellow volunteers, which she knew she'd never obtain by skulking around, sharing her thoughts with no one.

For the first time in Susannah's life, she paid attention to her hair, finding that, when she conditioned it with avocado, it fell into smooth, bouncy ringlets. The determined young lady also went on a strict diet, much to her father's grim satisfaction, and started working out in the beast's basement gym after school, taking great care to wipe down his equipment after-wards, to spare the wrath that would inevitably come if he knew that she had touched something that belonged to him.

Pounds melted away, revealing a figure that prompted more than one double-take from the boys who passed her in the hall. Susannah's overall appearance had changed dramatically in a matter of weeks, and she'd gone to a local thrift store in order to finish off her assimilation process by purchasing snug-fitting stylish jeans, low-cut tops like the other girls wore, and shoes that were the polar opposites of her sensible oxfords.

Between classes, she pilfered makeup, a curling iron and hair products from gym lockers, and spent hours in front of her mirror at home, teaching herself how to use them. Her mother would have been pleased to see the changes, if she hadn't been too busy to notice.

The morning of the athletic club breakfast dawned, cheery and bright, matching Susannah's disposition. She had waited and planned for weeks, and finally, the day had arrived. She dressed with extra care on that lovely morning, wearing a flattering outfit that would help her fit in with her peers until the deed was done. Once her revenge had been exacted without mercy, she could go back to being comfortable and fading into the woodwork socially.

Susannah checked in with Coach Nickerson in the cafeteria kitchen, noting with disdain the long looks that she was getting from people, boys in particular, who had never noticed that she lived and breathed prior to this morning. She put on a happy face however, and affected a cheerful demeanor much like the one that her mother adopted for parties and other social events. She smiled, she volunteered, she was quiet, but she was present, and she made certain that she had one of the serving positions.

Debbie Moran bounced into the cafeteria, shiny pony-tail swishing, with a cluster of lesser cheerleaders surrounding her. Susannah had known that her royal bitchness would be there with bells on, to accept what was rightfully hers. All of the high school elite had come out to be seen and appreciated by a fawning staff, and their inferior classmates. The annual break-fast practically existed to remind the lesser beings that they were fortunate to be allowed to attend the same institution of learning as these tanned, immaculate demi-gods.

Plating the fluffy hotcakes with care, while desperately hoping that Debbie Moran actually ate such things, Susannah loaded up a tray with several plates and delivered them to the table, setting each one down in front of the squad of debutants with a brilliant smile. Her mother would have been proud.

"Umm...helloooo," Debbie blinked at her in utter disbelief while dangling a pitcher of warm maple syrup from two perfectly manicured fingers.

A dark scenario suddenly flashed through Susannah's

mind, culminating in gelatinous goo bubbling from the cheerleader's eye socket after she stabbed a fork into that pretty blue orb, but she quickly quashed the thought and smiled.

"I'm sorry, is something wrong?" she asked sweetly, still savoring the brief image.

"Uh yeah," Debbie replied, clearly offended. "This may be enough syrup for everyone else, but I'm going to need my own pitcher. Don't be so stingy…how do you expect me to eat pancakes without enough syrup? I mean really, what would be the point?" she asked nasally, raising her eyebrows.

"Oh wow, of course," Susannah nodded. "I feel the same way," she smiled brightly. That part, at least, wasn't a lie. "Sorry about that, I'll be right back."

When she turned to head back to the kitchen, pleased that Debbie had played right into her hands, she heard the vile creature speak in a stage whisper that was clearly meant to be overheard.

"I swear, she's probably back there drinking the stuff," she snickered. "Soooey, Susannah, oink, oink, oink." The fact that Susannah had lost enough weight that her body now rivaled that of some of the cheerleaders surrounding their queen bee had apparently escaped Debbie Moran's notice.

Feeling the heat rise in her face, Susannah concentrated on taking some deep breaths and maintaining her mother's social façade. Her plan was almost complete. If she lost her cool now, she wouldn't have the satisfaction of seeing things through, so she collected her thoughts, pasted a lovely smile on her face and reached under the counter when no one was looking. She'd been force-fed syrup of ipecac often enough by her father, that she knew it's sweet taste was incredibly similar to thick maple syrup, and she had arrived early enough at the breakfast to have had time to prepare a special "syrup" just for dirty Debbie Moran, mixing in just a touch of maple syrup to mask the ipecac.

She stood in the kitchen, holding the pitcher for a moment, savoring what was about to happen, and wishing that she could film it, so that she could watch it over and over again, giggling all the while. Filming was out of the question however, for all sorts of reasons, so she'd just have to be content with having created a delightful amount of chaos and humiliation, and replaying it in her mind. She took a deep breath, and grinning broadly, she presented Debbie with her own personal pitcher of syrup, which the cheerleader poured liberally over her stack of pancakes. What happened after that would become a story that would be whispered about in the halls of the alma mater for years to come.

CHAPTER 2

Twenty-one year old Timothy Eckels was grouchy when he came home from his classes on that windy, wretched Fall afternoon – the afternoon where his life veered off course, and the part of him that was healthy and whole began to wither.

"I really hope you baked a pie today, Gram," he called out when he opened the front door of his grandmother's tidy little cottage. His cranky tone was not one that he ever directed at the matronly woman who raised him after his mother had died by her own hand, when her peculiar young son was only two. Gwendolyn Eckels had nurtured and brought up her odd, yet seemingly harmless, grandson with a firm but loving grace, and became the only person that Tim had found, as yet, who was deserving of his love.

The young man was baffled by the silence that greeted him, and grew even more peeved because of it.

"Gram!" he shouted, heading toward the kitchen, frustration evident in his voice.

When he reached the archway that led from living room to dining room, a chilly breeze caressed him with icy fingers, and his blood ran cold. Glancing across the kitchen, he saw the door to the back yard swinging open, crisp autumn air intruding into the cozy room. He stopped, somehow realizing that the next steps he took would be of a consequence that would haunt him to the end of his days. He didn't want to see, didn't want to know, but whatever unpleasantries awaited couldn't be avoided forever, so he allowed his feet, largely of their own accord, to propel him forward.

His darkest fears realized, he gazed down at his beloved Gram, her familiar thick body sprawled, in an ungainly manner that indicated a bad fall, on the back steps. Her apple-picking bowl, which she would have been carrying out to the trees in the back corner of the well-tended yard, was flung six feet to the side of her, and Tim absently wondered what sort of force could've propelled it that far. He couldn't breathe, and felt as though his heart had stopped in his chest. He knew she was dead, of that there was no question. No human form could be twisted in such a manner and have survived the event that left it so.

A mental shift happened so naturally that he didn't even notice it, and he didn't shed a tear for the only person he'd ever loved, but looked at her instead with a degree of curiosity that compelled him to action. He looked for blood and found none, making him curious as to how she had died instantly. No blood meant that she had been dead prior to her body impacting the steps, although her broken neck would've been the naturally assumed cause of death. She could've had a heart attack, he supposed, despite the fact that she'd had the energy and verve of a person half her age. Or perhaps it could've been a stroke that slammed through her brain, rendering her inanimate as she tried to go about picking her apples.

Tim sat on the step beside the husk of the woman who had raised him with tender, loving care, and gazed at the dark irises of her cerulean eyes, staring sightlessly skyward. Her skin was cold to the touch, feeling a bit like a fragile, squishy sack of goo, and he prodded her arm, just to see how far his finger would sink into her flesh.

Leaves skittered across the yard, and the young man without a grandmother shivered, not because of loss, but because the unrelenting breezes of Fall had brought the temperature of his skin down whilst he sat relatively motionless on the steps. Sighing at the unfortunate series of events that this occurrence would spur, he stood to his feet, bent over to pull Gram's skirt over her legs for modesty, and turned to go back in the house, not relishing the phone calls that he'd now have to make.

Gwendolyn Eckels was well-respected in the community, despite the strangeness of the grandchild that she'd raised. She had baked her famous pies for church socials, festivals and school events, and was known for her generosity and service toward friends, neighbors and strangers alike, so the turnout for her funeral was profound. Tim hadn't wanted to attend, preferring to avoid any event that involved a roomful of people with whom he'd have to make small talk, but the funeral director had insisted that the only remaining member of Gwen's family be present for the ceremony at the very least.

After the formalities, Tim was the last to file past the open casket that held the remains of his beloved Gram. He was astonished at the artistry with which the mortician had prepared her body – she looked as though she were merely sleeping - and in a brief moment of beautiful pain, her grandson had reached into the casket to brush back a lock of iron-grey hair from her forehead. There had been no fluffy white "old-lady" hair for Gwendolyn Eckels, she was made of sterner stuff, her hair as iron as her constitution. The unflappable lad gasped in abject horror as the skin beneath his hand slid a bit sideways, and the glue that held her eyelids shut pulled apart, revealing a sightless eyeball darkened by air exposure, covered with a plastic cap to give an appearance of roundness.

A fury mounted within Timothy Eckels, one of the last strong emotions that he'd ever experience. He was angry that her healthful appearance had deceived him for a moment, angry that the mortician had violated her shell with glue and stitches and whatever was producing the chemical smell that emanated from her flesh, and he was angry that the careless technician had screwed up. He wasn't meant to see the frailty of his grandmother's flesh, he wasn't meant to be left to live life without her, and she deserved better than to be hastily cobbled together by a worthless hack.

This butcher of the dead had made Tim attend an event that ground into his bones the cold reality of his grandmother's death, and in a moment of white hot anger, the young man charged at the tall, thin man in the pious black suit, bellowing in fury. He was restrained by the pall bearers who were waiting to close the lid and carry her to the death chariot that would take her to her planting place.

Advised by the sheriff, who had also attended the funeral, to avoid the graveside service, Tim, as usual, did as he pleased. He stood under a maple tree several yards away from the gravesite, while an officiant droned on, blazing red leaves sifting down around him as they lowered his Gram into the ground. The very next day, he enrolled in Mortuary School.

CHAPTER 3

Timothy Eckels hated group activities. He hated it when people carelessly brushed up against him, and hated the constant yammering that always seemed to happen when more than two people occupied a room. He was fortunate so far, because he'd been able to slip into the back of his classrooms without notice, taking notes and absorbing information, without having to actively participate. School was a means to an end – he needed an education in order to perform the very important task of properly preparing the dead, and if he could get through the educational process without having to speak to another human being, that would suit him just fine.

Cadaver Lab was the class that he'd been looking

forward to the most. It was the place where he'd finally get to experience working with cold, lifeless flesh for the first time, and he couldn't wait to get started. Walking into the sterile room with polished linoleum floors, he caught a whiff of formaldehyde and rubbing alcohol and his pulse sped up a bit. There were lab tables set up with spots for two people at each table, and when Tim spotted one that was entirely unoccupied, he made a beeline for it, dropping his notebook on the frigid metal and settling himself on his stool.

Students chattered around him, and he hoped that the vacant spot at his table would remain unoccupied, but alas, it was not to be. Just as the professor made his way to the front of the class, a chubby young blonde woman, clutching her backpack in front of her, made her way to the stool next to Tim, sitting down quickly and not looking at anyone. He sighed inwardly, but was glad that at least she had not attempted eye contact or conversation.

"Good afternoon ladies and gentlemen," the frazzle-haired man in a rumpled lab coat greeted them. "I'm Professor Soskowitz. If that's too much for you to handle, you may call me Professor Socks. Not box.

Not cocks. Socks. Are we clear on that?" he peered over his black spectacles, raising beetled eyebrows, as students tried to hide their surprised titters. Tim and the young woman next to him merely stared.

"Good then," he nodded, continuing. "This is a practical application course, so you will be working with human remains, beginning today. Your studies should have prepared you for this, and if you are unable or unwilling to conduct yourselves in a dignified manner in this lab, feel free to leave now," Socks challenged. "I'm sure they still have some openings in the Liberal Arts department," he rolled his eyes.

"No one? We're all adults here?" he confirmed, gazing at the class. "Good, then let's get started. Get to know the person with whom you're currently sitting, they will be your lab partner for the duration of this course," the professor instructed, causing Tim's stomach to drop to his shoes.

The introverted young man hazarded a glance at the blonde sitting next to him, only to find that she looked just as dismayed at the prospect of working together. They made awkward eye contact, their mouths attempting to form polite smiles, both failing miserably. Mercifully, the professor began speaking again, removing the need for further interaction.

"There are smocks in the closet at the rear of the room and boxes of nitrile gloves in the drawer under your tables. You have five minutes to prepare for today's lab, starting…now."

He deliberately drew back the sleeve of his coat and looked at his watch as students streamed toward the supply closet, passing Tim and his lab partner by.

Tim sighed and watched them climb over one another, scrambling to get their smocks and get back to their seats. He intended to wait until the frenzy had subsided, loathing the thought of being caught up in the fray, and apparently his lab partner was like-minded in that regard, standing behind her stool, watching, waiting. The two of them bided their time, then made their way to the closet, pulling the smocks on over their heads just as the professor began to speak. He reached down behind his desk and lifted up two buckets, which were filled with arms. Human arms.

When some of the students saw Professor Socks hoist

up the buckets and begin to move between the rows, allowing each team to select an arm to place on the cafeteria style tray that was in front of them, they had to work to suppress nervous giggles. The theory of handling a dead body was different than actually seeing a lifeless hand, nails chewed to the quick, on the cold metal table in front of you. The professor gave more than a few stern looks as he made his way around the classroom. His teaching assistant followed behind him, handing out packets of instructions to guide them through the lab.

Tim gently grabbed the hand nearest him when it was his turn. He found himself oddly fascinated by the bright pink manicured nails that were in nearly perfect condition on the curled fingers of the deceased, and pursed his mouth with regret when he saw the long slash on one wrist which had most likely been the cause of the woman's demise. He set the arm on their brown plastic tray carefully, almost reverently, not wanting to disturb the inanimate flesh, feeling the chill of it even through his gloves.

His lab partner pushed her glasses up her nose with a forefinger and bent closer to examine the upper arm, where it had been severed from the body.

"Hmm…sloppy," she murmured with a frown.

"Excuse me?" Tim couldn't help but blink at her in confusion.

"I'm a Culinary Arts major. The chickens we butcher are dissected with more precision than this," she explained, gesturing to the arm. "It's disgraceful."

Tim nodded, not quite understanding, but not wanting to have a conversation either. His lab partner went silent, suddenly focused on the table across the aisle from them, where two students were pulling various tendons in the arm to make the deceased's hand stick its middle finger up to "flip the bird," the universal symbol of contempt. They snickered quietly as they violated the remains with their frivolous behavior, and both Tim and his partner stared at them, aghast.

Timothy Eckels looked at the blonde woman by his side, seeing that she shared his dismay, and shook his head in disbelief.

"Barbarians," he whispered.

"Shameful," she replied.

"I'm Tim," he offered awkwardly.

"Susannah," was the quiet response.

"Nice to meet you," they said in unison, each of them looking down and blushing, relieved when the professor interrupted with some helpful hints, from the front of the room.

CHAPTER 4

Susannah trudged homeward, not looking forward to yet another evening spent enduring dinner with her parents, then doing homework until it was time for bed. The beast had made it quite clear that he would only fund her college education if she lived at home, so she'd stayed, despite the numerous escape fantasies she'd nurtured for the past several years of her miserable life.

Today, her step was a bit lighter than usual, oddly, and it was all because she'd been forced into interacting with someone, which she typically hated. Her lab partner, Tim, wasn't like the other students. He was a bit older for one thing, and didn't seem to care a bit about the frivolous things that most people in her classes nattered on about. When he looked at her, it seemed as if he saw a person, rather than a misshapen blob of humanity who had never quite fit in. Thick coke-bottle glasses magnified his warm brown eyes, and the way that his thin, lifeless hair fell over his forehead was rather endearing. He was the first person she'd met in a very long time who neither disgusted, nor infuriated her, and that made her feel a tiny bit exhilarated.

The beast and the china doll were having an argument when Susannah walked up the front steps and onto the porch. They lived in the country, so it took her two buses and a three mile walk to get home, but that meant that there was plenty of privacy when the perfect couple chose to go at each other's throats. She sighed, her hand on the knob, and barely caught snatches of their conversation. When she heard her name and the word tuition enter the argument, she figured it was time to interrupt.

"I'm home," she announced quietly, walking into the living room. The douchebag duo was in the kitchen, and she heard a moment of silence as they processed the fact that she was present.

"Susannah…" the beast looked her up and down, seeming as though he was trying hard not to sneer.

"You're going to have to drop out of school and get a job," he proclaimed, folding his perfectly tanned arms over his muscular chest.

"Honey, I'm sorry, it's just that we…" Greta began, looking pained and embarrassed. The beast cut her off before she could finish her sentence.

"No, don't apologize," he ordered, holding up a hand to silence her. He then turned his judgmental gaze toward their daughter. "You do chores around here, but it's not enough. You need to realize the value of good hard work, young lady. You need to start pulling your own considerable weight," he quipped nastily. Susannah had only gained back a fraction of the weight that she'd lost in high school, but she still disgusted the fitness-obsessed beast.

A rage so profound that it momentarily blinded her with a swimming miasma of red and purple, rose up within Susannah, and it took a considerable amount of self-control for her to maintain her composure. Her mind was made up in that instant. She would do what must be done. The beast saw an unattractive fat chick when he looked at his daughter, but what he didn't see was the clever and calculating mind behind those bespectacled eyes. She would make her way in the world, of that she was certain, and what that meant for him was yet to be determined.

"Fine," she replied without expression, and headed for her room.

The beast smirked, and her mother looked worried... as well she should.

Susannah dumped the remains of their "super food" dinner into the hog trough, absently noting that the pigs got to eat more of the expensive organic food, which her father insisted upon having, than she did. She was less resentful about that fact this evening however, because her mind was a million miles away, and when she finished slopping the pigs, she headed to her little woodshop in the goat barn. It didn't smell great in there, but she could create her wooden masterpieces in solitude, and the goats didn't care about the noise of various power tools.

She unrolled the Very Special Instruments that she kept hidden under a floor board, wrapped first in felt, to protect the shiny surfaces, then in plastic, to keep them safe from any barn-type substances which might make their way between the floor boards. She had worked hard for the money to procure these items over the internet, and opened up a post office box under a false name so that her parents couldn't intercept the packages when they came in. There were countless essays written on behalf of stupid or disinterested classmates, aluminum cans collected and taken to the recycling center, and even a stint working as a throaty phone-sex worker, which had allowed her to save the money that she needed to buy the Very Special Instruments.

Susannah's heart sped up a bit, as it always did when she first saw the glint of sublime metal after taking off the wrappings. She touched the VSI's lightly, affectionately, dreaming of the possibilities, then wrapped them back up with a sigh, whispering, "soon." Turning her attention to the tools which were displayed prominently above her workbench, she selected a handsaw and set it down on the well-worn surface. She had brought a stick of firewood with her, nothing special, just an ordinary piece of cord wood, which she cut in half. Carefully dusting off the blade of her saw and hanging it back up in its rightful spot, she then went to work on one of the halves of wood with a razor-sharp chisel.

Tapping on the end of the chisel lightly with a mallet, Susannah shaped and honed the wood until it resembled a very sharp railroad spike. It was roughly eight inches long and, at its thickest point, nearly two inches in diameter. Once the perfect size and shape had been achieved, she refined the piece further with a hand plane, then sanded it to a smooth, dull finish. She tapped a nail into the thick end of the spike and coated it entirely in polyurethane, then hung it to dry, with a string tied around the nail, out of sight, underneath the workbench.

The one thing that Susannah appreciated about her parents' strict adherence to routine was that it made their behavior much easier to predict. They went for an early morning jog every weekday, after which, her mother, Greta, would shower quickly and get out the door, while the beast went down to his basement gym to work the weights for precisely half an hour. He would then implement his morning cleansing ritual, after which, he'd drink a carefully measured protein shake, brush his teeth one more time, and head out the door.

Typically, Susannah would get up after the douchebag duo left for their run, and try to finish her chores, hurrying to prepare and eat her breakfast, so that she could hide the evidence of her consumption before they returned. For the past several mornings however, she'd had other tasks to accomplish. It was amazing the things that one could order from the internet, and after a couple of envelopes of cash had been sent to foreign countries, useful packets of a tasteless, but terribly toxic white powder had begun to appear, in discreet brown wrappings, in her post office box.

Susannah had been adding the arsenic, little by little to the beast's container of protein powder, and his condition had been worsening by the day. First he had nosebleeds, felt fatigued and experienced light nausea. As the days wore on, he started vomiting, and staying in the bathroom for long periods of time wracked with spasms of painful diarrhea.

There was one thing about the beast, Todd Guntzel-man, which would lead to his eventual demise... Todd took great pride in never being sick. He boasted of his extraordinary immune system, and Susannah had watched him suffer through various minor illnesses, while never for an instant admitting that he was ill. He never took over-the-counter meds, and he never went to a doctor. Ever. Which, of course, was perfect. Greta had tried to get him to go to the doctor this morning, but he'd responded with the excuse that he was merely choosing to sleep in because he was working too hard. He passed his vomiting and diarrhea off as a "part of his cleansing process," and shooed her out of the bedroom. Susannah watched with grim satisfaction as her mother closed the front door behind her, a worried frown on her lovely face.

The beast had lost the strength to even leave his bed, and when Susannah went in to check on him later, the stench before she even reached the door was overpowering. Though she had to breathe through her mouth to prevent her gag reflex from kicking in, she smiled a sinister smile at the thought of her father lying there in puddles of vomit and filth. He glanced up when she appeared in the doorway, his face grey, sweat beading on the sickly flesh.

"How are you feeling?" she taunted, holding her homemade spike behind her back. Her stomach churned at the sight and smell of him, but her heart beat faster with anticipation.

Todd's mouth gaped open as he tried to speak, a trail of bile leaking from the corner of his cracked lips.

Dehydration was a terrible thing. His eyes grew wide, and though he looked panicked, he was unable to utter more than an agonized grunt, and one hand flopped limply at his side as he tried in vain to gesture. It was time. Susannah advanced toward him, a faint smile playing about her lips. His expression of fear turned to one of resignation. He saw something in his fat, malevolent progeny that reminded him of his own dark soul, and he knew that the end had come. When she neared the bed, he closed his eyes and relaxed into his inevitability, never seeing the handcrafted spike that rocketed toward his torso.

Susannah quickly rolled her father onto his side after placing his limp hands around the spike. She'd been wearing nitrile gloves pilfered from the Cadaver Lab, so the only prints on the spike would be his. He was still alive, but had passed out, either from the pain or the poison, it didn't matter which, and by the time he could have even attempted to fight his way back to consciousness, he would have already bled out. She stood watching the rich red blood soak into the mattress, having lifted the spike out of the wound just enough to allow the coppery-smelling liquid to flow freely, and felt two emotions – relief and excitement.

Greta was horrified when she returned home for lunch

and found that her irascible, but wealthy husband had taken his own life. She wanted to keep his death quiet and refused an autopsy, despite his recent illness. Susannah was most supportive now that her mother had lost her partner and stood to collect on a massive insurance policy. Her mother felt that it would be best for her daughter to continue her education, so the chubby blonde returned to class the very next day... with a satisfied smile.

CHAPTER 5

It was dissection day in the Cadaver Lab, and Susannah volunteered to wield the scalpel.

"You're quite good at that," Timothy Eckels observed with quiet admiration.

"Years of practice," was the cryptic reply.

"On what?"

"Chickens, pigs, goats, fish, and a whole lot of other foods in my culinary courses," Susannah shrugged, slicing deftly through precisely the right amount of skin and fat without disturbing nerves and vessels.

"Do you have to kill them first?"

"Who?" she asked absently, focused on the task at hand.

Tim stared at her for a moment, thinking that "who" had been a strange response to his question.

"The…uh…animals. Before you…dissect them," he blinked rapidly behind his thick-lensed glasses.

Susannah gave him a lopsided grin.

"Well, it's kind of difficult to filet something that's still walking around," she teased, enjoying the way that the perfectly-sharpened knife slipped through the cold flesh like butter.

Tim smiled back awkwardly, paying close attention to her cuts.

"Hey, wait," he lightly touched the back of her hand to still the cutting motion.

"What?" she frowned, seeming offended. "This is how this is supposed to be done…" Susannah began to protest, but trailed off when she saw Tim peering more intently at the flesh in front of them.

"Look at this…" he whispered.

"What is it?" she pushed her glasses up with the back of her wrist.

"Tweezers," he commanded. Susannah didn't hesitate, grabbing them from the tray and handing them over.

Parting the folds of skin that she'd just sliced open, he carefully inserted the tweezers, and started pulling them out, ever so gently, bringing a long, thin white worm with them.

"Congratulations, Table 8, I was wondering if any of you would be sharp-eyed enough to find the parasitic worms that had infested this unfortunate young man before his death," Professor Socks boomed, startling both Tim and Susannah, who had been so intent upon their work that they'd forgotten that anyone else was even in the room.

The duo didn't know how to react, so they simply stared blankly at him, with Susannah holding the scalpel and Tim holding tweezers with a pallid worm dangling from them.

"Well done," Socks nodded. "Carry on."

"You're good at this," Susannah looked at Tim as though seeing him for the first time.

"Thanks," he replied, staring back.

"I'd like to cook for you," she said simply.

"I make pies," Tim set the tweezers with the worm down carefully on the tray.

"Then you should come to my house," her eyes followed the tweezers, the worm. "I'll cook for you, and you bring a pie for me."

"Yes," he nodded.

Timothy Eckels stood on Susannah's front porch, holding a Key Lime Pie. He pushed the doorbell and heard it clanging within the contemporary "farm" house. The imposing structure was a far cry from his humble apartment, but he was so focused on listening for approaching footsteps that he hardly noticed.

"You brought a pie," she said when she opened the door.

"My grandmother made the best pies," he offered gravely.

"My grandmothers live in Florida. Come in."

She opened the door wider and stepped back so that he could enter. They were both wearing the same clothes that they had worn to school, and Tim, as usual, hadn't bothered to comb his thinning hair. The interior of the home was well-kept and sparsely furnished, looking somewhat like an ad for an upscale furniture store, and smelled of cleanser. It was a strange contrast to the older buildings behind the home, which housed farm animals of all sorts and surrounded an organic vegetable garden.

"This is your house?" Tim asked, blinking at Susannah and still holding his pie.

"No, this is my mother's house," she shrugged, sending a lightning bolt of terror rippling through him. He hadn't anticipated having to deal with a stranger, and was quite certain that he wouldn't be able to eat in front of Susannah's mother.

"Where is she?" he choked out the words.

"Somewhere in the Caribbean, why?" she looked at him curiously.

"There might not have been enough food," he glanced away.

"Oh don't worry, I made plenty. I hope you're hungry," she took the pie and put it in the fridge.

"Why would you hope that?" Tim was baffled.

For the first time in quite a while, Susannah actually smiled. A good, healthy, tooth-exposing smile appeared like the sun coming out of the clouds and Tim was caught off guard, staring.

"Because then you'll enjoy my food more," she continued grinning. "And still have room for pie."

"Oh. Well then, yes, I'm hungry," he nodded, still somewhat dazed by her smile.

"Good. Here, you can open the wine and put it on the table in there," she directed, handing him a bottle of expensive red wine that had been in her late father's collection, and a corkscrew.

Tim looked at the corkscrew curiously.

"Do you know how to use that?" Susannah asked.

"Yes," he avoided her eyes.

"Good. I'll meet you in there with the food in a few minutes," she said, turning back toward the stove, where something that smelled delicious was burbling in a pot.

Tim took the wine and the corkscrew to the dining room, where the table had been set for two, and regarded the corkscrew with trepidation. He'd never seen anything like it in his entire life. His grandmother had never indulged in spirits, and he'd never so much as tasted a drop of wine. Susannah came in from the kitchen bearing a platter of crusty, golden-brown garlic bread that was liberally sprinkled with herbs and parmesan.

"Just set that down on the table," she instructed, seeing that he hadn't yet opened the wine. "I'll open it in a minute."

She returned moments later with two heaping plates of spaghetti and meatballs, setting one down on each placemat. Sitting down, she took the wine and opened it, while Tim watched, fascinated.

"Do you like wine?" she asked, reaching for his glass.

"I don't know."

"You've never had it before?"

He shook his head.

"Well, this one pairs really well with the spices in the food, so it should taste really good," she assured him, pouring a glass for each of them.

Tim thanked her and picked up his fork, spearing a meatball and taking a bite. He chewed slowly, enjoying the flavors, then frowned.

"This meatball…it's really good, but it tastes…different," he admitted.

"Oh, that's just George," Susannah shrugged, placing a hunk of garlic bread on the side of his plate.

"George?" he asked, quietly putting down his fork.

"One of our calves. The meatballs are made from veal," she explained, twining strands of pasta around the tines of her fork.

"Do you always eat food that used to have a name?"

"Around here…usually," she nodded.

"What do you do with the parts that you don't eat?" he asked.

"I'll show you after dinner. Are you going to try the wine?"

"Okay," he replied, reaching out and awkwardly grabbing the glass by the stem, trying to imitate the way that Susannah held hers.

He brought the glass to his lips and sipped, making an awful face.

"I think it's gone bad," he gasped, hurriedly drinking from his water glass.

Susannah grinned again, delighted.

"You don't like it," she observed with approval. "It's a three thousand dollar bottle from my father's collection, and you think that it tastes bad."

"I would think that three thousand dollars would taste better," Tim grimaced.

"Timothy, I don't like people, generally, but I think we're going to get along just fine," Susannah proclaimed.

"I'd say so," he nodded.

Tim had never been to a barn in his life, but this one would have held surprises even if he had been accustomed to the drafty buildings filled with straw and animals. Susannah had taken him to the chicken coop, the pigpen, and the cowshed, finally leading him here, to the far end of the goat barn. Beside her workbench, there was a strange tree with paper-thin leaves that rustled from their oddly white branches. Scattered on shelves around the bench were sculptures made from wood and other materials, which were creative and quite good.

"You're an artist," Tim observed, his eyes traveling from one piece to the next while she watched him taking it all in.

"I guess," she shrugged.

"This is how you're so precise with your cuts. You work with your hands, you know how tools work, you have skills."

"It's my escape," she admitted, her eyes downcast.

"You make the animals into art," Tim's eyes peered into her soul from behind those coke-bottle glasses.

Susannah nodded, wondering at the fact that she saw no judgment at all in his gaze. He missed nothing. His eye for detail had seen that the leaves on the trees were made from the skins of various types of animals, and the branches were long, polished bones. Her sculptures included bits of bone, leather, teeth, claws and fur. Nothing was jagged, or ragged, or torn, everything was precisely cut, honed and placed to achieve a spectacular, if macabre balance.

"It's perfect," he murmured, his eyes shifting from her, back to her artistry.

She had the same reverence for the preservation and presentation of flesh that had compelled him to go to mortuary school in the first place. She understood. She was as much of an oddity to the outside world filled with "normal" people as he was. Tim had found someone with whom he could relate, for the first time since his beloved Gram had passed.

"I should go," he said after a long moment.

"I'll walk you to your car," Susannah reached for his hand, and he let her take it.

When they got to the car, she let his hand go and gazed up at him, studying his face, his eyes.

"You should kiss me goodnight," she said matter-of-factly.

"Why?" Tim blinked at her curiously.

"Because this is a date and that's what happens."

"Oh."

He stood, staring at her, not uncomfortable at all, but clearly not knowing what to do next.

"Here," she said approaching him and putting her hands on his shoulders. "Bend down toward me a bit and close your eyes," Susannah directed.

"Really?"

"Yes. That'll get it started," she nodded.

"Okay," he agreed, and did as he was told.

Susannah stood on her tiptoes and brushed her lips quickly against his, startled at the rush of feeling that the simple action had sent spiraling through her.

Tim stayed put, eyes still closed.

"You can open your eyes now."

"Was that right?" he asked.

She nodded, staring up at him.

"I had a nice time, Tim. Thank you for the pie."

"You're welcome," he couldn't take his eyes from hers for some reason. "My Gram..." he began.

"Always made the best pies," Susannah finished for him.

"Yes," he nodded. "See you tomorrow."

"Tim, you won't tell anyone about my...art, will you?" she whispered.

"People don't talk to me," he shrugged.

CHAPTER 6

Tim and Susannah chatted regularly before class and after, and he'd visited the farm for dinner more than once, since her mother seemed to stay gone as much as possible. Susannah was the first person since his Gram with whom he'd felt comfortable enough to share conversation, even bestowing a rare smile upon her on occasion. She understood what it was like to feel shunned by the rest of the world. Tim had been abandoned by his parents, and Susannah had wished her whole life to be abandoned by hers. They'd both been the objects of ridicule and scorn from their class-mates, and even teachers on occasion, and both had simply turned silently inward to hide from the pain of alienation. Tim had at least had Gram, Susannah had no one...until now.

Today's lab was exciting for both of them, though for entirely different reasons. It was head and neck day, and Tim was eager to see the effects of death on important tissues and organs that would affect how a body was prepared for funeral presentation. Susannah was glad that she'd finally be able to wield the bone saw, peeling back the scalp and penetrating the skull to uncap the brain. She hadn't killed anyone or anything since Todd had taken his last painful breath, and there was a nearly constant buzzing in the back of her brain that compelled her to seek out flesh to cut. Cadaver Lab was keeping her community safe for the moment, but the rush of power that she'd felt when taking a life, be it man or animal, was a heady sensation that she longed to experience again…and soon.

Susannah thrilled at being the one in control, the one who decided whether someone or something was allowed to live, or whether they should die. Every slight, every snicker, every carelessly rude comment that had ever been visited upon her, flashed through her brain as a dark reminder of the relief that was to be found in the cold sharp steel of knives and saws and picks. Tim found his satisfaction in turning cold, dead flesh into something that looked like a healthy vital human being who was merely taking a nap among the folds of satin in their coffin. They were both perfectionists in their own way, him making certain that the body was prepared perfectly, leaving loved ones with a pristine image of the deceased, and her deftly applying her instruments with the appropriate amount of malice needed to punish whomever she saw fit to kill. She was merciful with animals. They gave their lives to sustain her, in more ways than one, so she did all that she could to minimize their fear and pain.

When the tray with the homeless man's head was placed in front of them, Susannah's eyes widened. Tim noted her response and tried his awkward best to provide comfort, knowing that Professor Socks would not be pleased if she freaked out over a dead head.

"It's okay," he whispered, trying not to move his mouth much. "He looks like he didn't have a happy life anyway."

Susannah continued to stare at the head numbly, but nodded. Tim was surprised, he'd never known his lab partner to be squeamish before. She was accustomed to severed heads, having lived on a farm, but perhaps the fact that this was a human head bothered her for some unfathomable reason.

"Do you want me to do the dissection this time?" he offered.

The look that she shot him when he said that seemed like desperation mixed with anger.

"No," she said quietly. "Just hold it in place and I'll do it."

Professor Socks moved about the classroom watching the progress at various tables and stopping to comment occasionally. He usually glided by Tim and Susannah, not knowing quite what to make of the clearly intelligent, but awfully strange duo. Today however, he paused, watching as Susannah made her scalp incisions like a pro. Tim bent one wax-filled ear forward and shuddered in revulsion when he saw the corpses of dead lice piled in the crease behind the ear.

"Interesting," Socks mused, moving closer.

Tim heard Susannah's breathing quicken and figured that she must be nervous because of the professor's scrutiny.

"What's interesting?" Tim asked. Immediately curious, he craned his neck and moved closer, trying to get a better look.

Timothy Eckels firmly believed that each inanimate body had a story to tell, and that it was just a matter of looking closely enough to find out what that story might be. He'd picked up on several things during the class that had impressed and astounded his teacher.

"Look there," Socks pointed with one gloved finger to a space that had been hidden by the man's ear. There was a patch of skin which had been cleanly cut out, that resembled a capital D.

Timothy frowned. "What would have caused that?" he murmured.

"That is deliberate," Socks replied. "It looks almost surgical."

"Is there a procedure that requires that kind of cut?" Tim's typical reticence in speaking to people was overcome by his fascination with the body.

"Not that I'm aware of," the professor raised an eyebrow. "Even removal of a tumor would've gone much further below the surface."

"I did it," Susannah whispered.

Tim stared at her, befuddled. He'd been there with her the whole time and knew that she hadn't made the cut.

"The knife must've slipped when I was about to make an incision," she continued, blushing furiously.

"Nonsense, my dear," Socks shook his head. "This incision is old. Can you explain to me how I know that it's an old incision, Mr. Eckels?" he asked, as a couple of students at nearby tables watched, mildly interested.

"Because there's decomposition on the edges. It's faint, but it's there. The incision happened post mortem, but it happened before the body was discovered or processed," Tim replied, leaning so close to the cut that if he'd have stumbled, his nose would have landed in the corpse's filthy ear.

"Very good, Mr. Eckels," Socks nodded. "And don't worry, Miss Guntzelman, it's an easy mistake to make, but rest assured, you did not mutilate this corpse," he chuckled.

She stared at the professor for a moment until Tim subtly nudged her with his knee.

"Okay," she nodded, and went back to the task at hand.

"Proceed," Socks said, frowning at her odd behavior, but moving on.

"Are you…okay?" Tim said in a low voice.

"Of course, why wouldn't I be?" she replied, never looking up from her work.

"Umm…okay. Good." He was actually relieved that she seemed to be fine now, a nurturer he was not. He hated any sort of strong emotion and would have had no idea as to how to comfort her.

The buzzing in Susannah's brain grew louder and louder, so much so that she had to work hard to achieve perfection in her cuts on the corpse. Adrenalin surged through her and she concentrated hard on keeping her hands from shaking. She had made the cut behind the man's ear, shortly after she had severed his carotid, just below his other ear, under a bridge in a bad part of town. After his lifeblood had stopped flowing, she had claimed her prize…another leaf of skin for the tree in her workshop. She'd taken his baby toe for good measure, just to use in a sculpture.

It hadn't been a particularly sweet death. Since it was in public, she hadn't been able to savor his earthly departure for very long, but it had stilled the buzzing…for a while.

CHAPTER 7

"Do you really think we're going to like it here?" Susannah Eckels asked her husband, timidly pushing her heavy glasses up with the back of her hand, after setting down the small moving box that she had brought into their new home.

"I think we'll be fine," Tim, replied noncommittally, seemingly distracted by the task at hand. The plump, blond woman sighed and headed back out to the moving truck that they had rented after deciding to open a mortuary in the small town of Pellman, Minnesota.

The house that they bought was literally right next door to the sprawling Victorian which served as mortuary and funeral home, so Tim's commute consisted simply of walking from the kitchen door of his house, through a break in a hedge and onto the side porch of Eckels Funeral Home. There were a series of tile-lined rooms, along with cold-storage, in the basement, Tim's most favorite part of the once-grand home. The main floor featured a small chapel, three separate viewing rooms, and a mortician's office where family members of the deceased could meet with him to select caskets, floral arrangements and service plans. The reclusive mortician hoped to someday soon be able to hire someone to take care of the interactive end of his business, so that he could focus solely on the dead, a task with which he was supremely more comfortable.

In the tiny town, where jobs were often hard to come by if one hadn't been born and raised there, shy, secretive Susannah had been fortunate to land a job as a chef's assistant in Pellman's only fine dining estab-lishment, Le Chateau. She'd accepted the job after an interview over the phone with the head chef, never having "met" the man himself. The quiet, unassuming woman was understandably nervous about her new job, but had complete confidence that her brave and focused husband would succeed as Pellman's only local mortician and funeral director. Once he'd carved his niche in the town, he'd be able to hire someone to handle all of the things about the business that made him uncomfortable, and they'd be able to live their calm, sedate life without stress and distraction. Susannah had been able to keep her bloodlust down to an acceptable level by distracting herself with cooking, but days spent on the road to Pellman had taken their toll, and she was beginning to squirm with need, her fingers twitching for a polished blade.

The couple unrolled a worn Persian rug which had been a keepsake from Gram's house, put their nondescript taupe chenille sofa on top of it, arranged lamps, a coffee table and small dinette set in the living area of their newly purchased cottage, and called it a day. Exhausted from the move, they slept on a mattress in the Master bedroom because neither of them had the energy to set up the bed frame. There was none of the usual excitement of moving into a new community, or beginning a new life, just a pragmatic realization that there was much to be done and only the two of them to do it.

Tim and Susannah's relationship had morphed into a symbiotic organism, bringing with it the comfort of familiarity, yet each of them spent much of their existence puzzling through the mysteries of life within the confines of their own heads. Evenings together were often spent without a word being exchanged until it was time for a polite "good night." Neither of them longed for an exciting, eventful, or passionate union, and found contentment in the predictability of their daily routine. Meal times were scheduled, household tasks divided, and free time was typically spent alone, even when in the same room.

When they awoke that first morning in Pellman, they went about their individual tasks, much as they always had. Tim was next door in the mortuary, making certain that the tools of his trade were organized in an efficient manner, and Susannah, who didn't have to report to work until the following day, spent her time organizing the house and breaking down boxes to leave out for recycling. She had brought her art with her, along with the instruments of her darker hobby, and set up an elaborate workshop in the basement of their new home. She kept her bloody passions to herself, liking Tim too much to have to kill him if he dared to share her secrets.

Tim hadn't been in the mortuary for more than an hour, fussing with his instruments, preparation agents and potions, when the phone in the office rang, shattering his peaceful process. He had mixed feelings about answering the call. On the one hand, picking up the receiver meant interacting with a human being, which was not high on his list of enjoyable practices. On the other hand, the call might also provide an opportunity to practice his craft, and that's why he had come to Pellman.

"Eckels Mortuary," he answered, finally picking up the phone.

Jackpot - he had a body. The mortician repressed a smile, knowing that excitement in such a situation was not societally acceptable, and he always tried to maintain some semblance of normalcy, even in private, it was simply good practice. Jotting down the details of how to get to the remote site, Tim snagged the keys to his classic black hearse, and headed out the back door of the forest-green fishscale Victorian with a renewed spring in his step.

Timothy Eckels wasn't surprised to find that the house to which he'd been summoned was a giant, imposing brick mansion, nestled in the woods, behind iron gates and a brick wall that were at least ten feet high. Wealthy folks died just as often as poor ones did, and the financial status of the deceased didn't interest him in the slightest, provided that they could pay his fees. When his hearse approached the gates, they swung open as though someone had been watching for his arrival. He looked up and saw cameras on both sides of the gate, wondering what lay beyond the thick mahogany doors of the mansion.

Picking up a new corpse never failed to stimulate his creativity, although he preferred the challenges to his skill that were presented in the instances of violent death. He could patch, sew and glue a body back together more seamlessly than anyone else in his graduating class, and had been offered a position with the finest mortuary in town upon completion of his courses. He'd grown and thrived in his craft, and the decision to go out on his own had been an easy one.

His pulse raced a bit as he grabbed his bag from the passenger seat and headed toward the mansion. The door opened just as he reached up to knock on it, and he stood face to face with Arlen Bemis, the local sheriff.

"You Eckels?"

"I am," Tim nodded.

"I need to speak with you right quick," the sheriff

announced, hitching up his gun belt with extreme self-importance, and stepping outside, closing the solid wood door behind him.

He leaned in close, as though thinking he might be overheard, and tapped gently on Tim's chest with two fingers.

"Listen up Eckels," Arlen ordered sternly. Tim just blinked at him, wishing he'd hurry up so that he could get inside and see the body. "What we got here is a bit of a situation," the sheriff jerked a thumb back toward the house. "The deceased was a very prominent man here in town, and the way I see it, it ain't nobody's business how he died, you understand that, Eckels?"

"Not really, Sheriff…no," Tim admitted, thinking that he'd actually been asked a question.

"Well ain't you just a smarty pants," Bemis grimaced. "Then let me break it down to you nice and easy. You get in there and you do whatever you gotta do to make him look like he's in a deep sweet sleep, and keep your mouth shut about the way he died. You get it that time?" he growled.

Tim was utterly baffled, never having encountered this type of situation before. "Okay," he replied slowly, hoping that was the answer that the sheriff was looking for.

Success. The sheriff clapped him on the shoulder hard enough to make him stagger forward a bit.

"Good, I just knew you'd be the understandin' type," he smiled nastily. "Now, get on in there and do what you gotta do." The sheriff gestured toward the door, and, not knowing what else to do, Tim opened it and slipped inside.

Arlen Bemis strode past him. "This way," he said, moving toward a hall to the right of a massive marble foyer.

A couple of turns and an elevator ride to the third floor later, the sheriff gravely led Tim into a master bedroom that was the size of most single family homes, and he finally caught a glimpse of the deceased, who was laying on his back on the bed. The reason that the sheriff had insisted upon the odd conversation was immediately clear. The man on the bed had hung himself.

Standing beside the stainless steel slab where most of the dirty work of preparing the dead was done, Tim crossed his arms and gazed at the body, frowning. He had heard of such things, but had never actually believed that people did them, and now, he was in a quandary as to what to do about what he had discovered. It was common practice for him to prevent leakage of bodily fluids after embalming by placing an absorbent powder-filled plug in the rectum of the deceased. When he had attempted to do so for this particular corpse, he had discovered the disturbing fact that the man had apparently been raped.

Trying to be diligent, he photographed the evidence that he found – smears of dried blood, anal fissures, and an overly stretched rectum, and documented his discovery to report to the police later. When he did an internet search regarding the anal violation, he also discovered the source of the strange marks which had been present on the victim's face. Apparently something called a ball-gag had been used. Timothy Eckels was fairly innocent when it came to matters of the heart and bedroom, and had never heard of the term "autoerotic asphyxiation," but when he read the description of it, he was fairly certain that the deceased had succumbed while experiencing it.

Tim filled out a form to turn into the sheriff's office after he finished preparing the body. His phone had been ringing off the hook with concerned citizens asking about what time the services were, and where they should donate or send flowers. There were even calls from local news agencies wondering if Tim could add anything to the account that they'd been given by the family. He'd ignored the phone, doing what he needed to do for the deceased, and intended to go to the sheriff's office after the preparation was complete.

Arlen Bemis stared across the desk at Tim, refusing to touch the report that the mortician was holding out to him.

"I thought that I had made myself fairly clear in this matter, Mr. Eckels. Nothing, and I mean NOTHING is to be said about this death. Now which part of that don't you understand?" he hissed, squinting furiously at his closed office door.

"But he was violated in what must have been an awful…" Timothy began, blinking rapidly in the face of such hostility.

The sheriff held up a hand to interrupt. "I don't care what he may have experienced in his personal life. None of this matters, got it?" He stood up and leaned into Tim's face until they were nearly nose to nose. "This old boy was the governor's brother, and if you even think about saying anything about his death to anyone, I'll make sure you're run outta this town, hell, this state, on a rail, are you hearing me, Eckels? You'll wish you were never born," he snarled.

With that, Bemis snatched the report from Tim's hand, tore it in half and in half again and tossed it in the waste basket. "Not another word about this, got it?"

Tim nodded, mouth hanging slightly open in disbelief.

"Good, now get the hell outta here and I better never hear from you on this again," the sheriff sat back down, and as soon as Tim was out of the office, he picked up the phone.

CHAPTER 8

Susannah glared at Jorge, the prep cook, the weight of a large silvery knife in her hand, tempting her with its delightfully sharp blade. She noted that the beautifully bronzed skin of the twenty-something Hispanic man would make a lovely rust-colored leaf for her trophy tree, and licked her lips, savoring the thought. He seemed to delight in frustrating her with uneven cuts, haphazard measures, and a generally lackadaisical approach to the art of creating the perfect dish. His latest offense had been cutting vegetables that were supposed to be perfectly julienned. In his haste to get out the door for a Friday night adventure, the handsome young buck had quickly sliced the veggies into strips of varying widths, lengths and thicknesses. This was NOT acceptable in Susannah's world, and her hand tightened a fraction on the knife.

"Just go," she told the charming, grinning young man in a quiet voice.

Go now…before I decide to show you how to julienne by using your own flesh as an example, her mind intoned darkly. She'd have to quickly julienne the vegetables herself. Fortunately, her knife skills would make that a relatively easy task. She watched Jorge dart gratefully out the back door toward whatever inane activity awaited him, and threw his tray of vegetables down the garbage disposal. The urge to spill his blood rose up within her, filling her senses, and she literally had to bite the inside of her cheek, hard, to cause the feeling to ebb a bit. The coppery taste of her own blood in her mouth sent an electric thrill through her.

It had been a long time since she'd taken a human life. She had to be very careful in their new home, it was a small town, where such things might be noticed, but the itch to control life and death was becoming harder and harder to resist. She envied her husband in that he delighted in processing bodies that were already dead, which was far more socially acceptable than her need to extinguish the human spark that animated even the most vile bags of flesh.

Susannah always tried to wait until she happened upon someone who deserved to die...men who lived to control, men like her father, Todd. The profound relief that she'd felt after watching his organic-fed blood ooze from him in time with his sluggish heartbeat, clued her in to the idea that she should focus her hobby on those who tormented either her, or others, with their need for dominance and control. Jorge fit the bill somewhat nicely, because he used his bright white teeth and good looks in order to manipulate those around him, pretending to flirt, even with her. She'd give it more thought though, because he generally seemed rather nice. She sighed and turned her full attention to the vegetables – there was work to be done.

Timothy Eckels had enjoyed a steady flow of business after moving to Pellman, and aside from the strange initial encounter with the sheriff, his experiences with the locals had been unremarkable. He was in the basement working on the hair of a recently deceased matron when a buzzer alerted him to the fact that someone had come in. He sighed, not simply because he'd have to pull off his gloves, put the deceased back in her drawer, and come back later to finish up, but also because he now had to do the part of his job that he hated – he had to talk to someone.

Tim trudged up the stairs, reminding himself not to grumble out loud, and saw a young mother with a baby in her arms and a toddler at her side. The toddler had all four fingers of one hand in his mouth, sucking on them, and the mortician tried not to shudder.

"May I help you?" he asked, surprised to see someone young and healthy-looking in his velvet-curtained realm.

"Hi," the woman looked nervous, and Tim cocked his head, waiting. "My name is Shelby Myers, you did my cousin Sally's funeral a couple of months ago, you probably don't remember me, but it was very nice," she began.

A memory flashed through Tim's mind. He remembered Sally. She'd been in a car crash, and he'd had to make a wax replica of the bones in her face in order to reconstruct her well enough to be seen in an open casket. The job had been a delightful challenge, and his work had been flawless.

"Yes, of course. I remember Sally," he replied truthfully.

"Is there…uh…someplace that we can sit down and talk for a minute?" Shelby asked, looking around as though she was afraid of being followed or overheard.

Tim died a little inside. He had a feeling that this wasn't going to be a quick and easy casket quote.

"Certainly. Follow me," he led the way to the spotless office where he met with those who were shopping for caskets and funeral services. "What is it that you'd like to talk about?" he asked, clasping his hands in front of him after settling into his desk chair.

Shelby Myers pulled some toys out of a large tote and placed them on the floor in the corner of the office, instructing the toddler to play for a few minutes. When she sat down in one of the chairs across the desk from Tim, the baby that she'd been carrying sat in her lap, patting little pink hands on the highly polished mahogany. The mortician blinked at the tiny human, thinking that he'd have to polish the desk top after the woman left.

"I feel really strange coming here to talk to you about

this," she began, looking embarrassed. "But I'm at my wit's end and I just don't know where else to turn."

Tim frowned, wondering what on earth she could possibly want. "Go on," he encouraged warily.

"Our cat, Bootsie, is really old, and really sick," she explained, lowering her voice and glancing over at the toddler, who was seemingly entranced by a pop-up book about trains. "The vet said that if we just gave her the right supplements, she'd be fine. He has this really expensive line of supplements that are supposed to be the best thing ever, but they're not working," she bit her lip.

"I'm sorry to hear that," Tim replied, using the line that he'd been taught in mortuary school. It was a good, solid, seemingly sympathetic response that could be used whenever someone was expressing grief or discomfort and it had served him well in the past.

"Thank you," Shelby sighed, looking uncomfortable. "So, she's getting worse instead of better…and I even asked the vet to…" she glanced over her shoulder again and whispered, "…put her down."

Tim nodded, wishing that he had somewhere else to be.

"Because she's suffering, you know? And I can't stand watching the suffering."

Having exhausted his supply of supportive responses, the mortician simply blinked at her.

"I'm sorry, I can do small caskets for animals, but it's quite costly, and I don't believe that most cemeteries will allow you to inter pets," he put on his professionally kind mortician face.

"Oh, no, that's not why I'm here," Shelby had begun absently stroking the fine, wispy hair atop her baby's head.

"Oh?" Tim was befuddled.

"The vet said no," she confided, leaning in a bit.

"Okay."

"That's why I'm here."

"I don't understand."

"Well, I know that because of the kind of work that you do, you might have access to certain chemicals and things, and I hoped that maybe you'd be able to help me out with my...situation," Shelby said in a rush, her eyes downcast, cheeks aflame.

Tim's eyebrows shot up to his hairline.

"Are you asking me to...?"

"She's suffering, please...I don't know where to go or what to do," her eyes filled with tears and sweat beaded in tiny dots on her forehead.

"I work with those who are already dead when they get here."

"I know, but...your wife has small animals that she raises for food, doesn't she? Would she maybe know of some humane way to...you know...?"

Tim stared at the young woman in front of him, feeling a bit ill. He had no problem working with life-less flesh, but the thought of taking a life, even a feline one, turned his stomach a bit.

"I..." he started to demur, but she reached a hand across the desk, placing it palm down in front of him, pleading.

"Please...can you at least ask her, or think about the

chemical thing? Please? I wouldn't have come, but I can't stand it anymore, I really can't," Shelby begged, her eyes filling with tears.

One thing that Tim had never been able to handle was tears, particularly in the eyes of a sweet, young female. He looked down at the hand on the desk in front of him.

"I'll talk to her," he sighed.

CHAPTER 9

Jorge had been late for the last two days in a row, creating extra work and stress for Susannah, and the worst part was that he thought he could erase all ill will by smiling that dazzling smile. The head chef loved Susannah's work because it was always precise and always perfect. He had the creativity to imagine the dish, and she had the discipline to craft it in exactly the manner that he described. Jorge was a thorn in her side because his tardiness messed with her schedule and her insistence upon perfection. Her fingers itched to snip off several large leaf-shaped pieces of his skin. Any guilt that she might have felt about wanting to flay him from stem to stern with her filet knife was quashed when she considered his potential impact upon her performance as an assistant

chef. The more he tried to flirt his way out of conse-
quences, the closer he came to being turned into
various pieces of art.

Susannah glanced up from the chicken that she was
boning to see the smarmy grin on Jorge's face as he
brought over a tray of breadcrumbs that he had just
grated for the chicken batter. Her blood boiled when
she saw the uneven chunks and pieces on the tray. The
crumbs were an abomination, and she took a breath as
a consuming red rage brewed within her chest.

"Here you go, chica," he grinned, setting the tray next
to her, his hands resting on the counter.

One quick chop of the cleaver that was in her hand,
and she'd have four new appendages to include in a
sculpture. Her fingers twitched with want, the cleaver
heavy in her grip. She raised her head, leaving the
cleaver on the joint between the chicken's leg and
thigh.

"The crumbs need to be more even in their consisten-
cy," she said calmly, having spent a lifetime learning
how to appear normal, even when she was seething
inside.

"Ah, come on…what difference does it make, it all gets smashed down in the pan anyway," he wheedled, edging into Susannah's personal space, and setting her teeth even more on edge.

She refused to step back, knowing that he was trying to manipulate her by getting too close. When she turned to speak to him, his face was so close to hers that she could smell what he'd had for dinner. His lips were perfectly kissable, soft and full, and all that Susannah could think of was what they'd look like after drying out in her dehydrator for a couple of weeks.

"It makes a difference," she said tonelessly, staring into his long-lashed brown eyes. "Re-do them and get it right this time."

Jorge touched his tongue to his teeth, bringing on his hottest techniques to try to melt the iceberg in front of him, and Susannah had a strange desire to turn the pink organ into a specialty dish.

"Don't be so upset, beautiful," he ran his fingers lightly along the back of her upper arm, raising goosebumps, which he took to be a good sign. It wasn't. "It's just bread crumbs," he husked, eyeing her mouth.

Susannah employed every bit of willpower that she had within her to hold back from using a melon baller to scoop out his eyes.

"They're not just bread crumbs, Jorge, they're part of the foundation of the dish, and as such, are important," she glared at him, not budging an inch.

"Susannah!" she heard a shout from behind her that made her jump, and turned to see Andre, the head chef, standing, hands on hips, eyes narrowed suspiciously as he took in the scene in front of him. "Where are we on those chickens? We've got a full house tonight," he reminded her sternly.

He shouldn't have done that, no matter what he thought he saw. She didn't like it when men spoke to her sternly. Bad things happened when men talked to her sternly. Things that offered a permanent solution to their control issues...

Susannah crouched outside Jorge's house, thinking

how handy it had been that there were huge evergreen bushes next to the shabby structure. It made for a scratchy but fragrant wait. She'd been plotting for weeks now, biding her time and pretending to be nice to the prep cook so that he'd be as shocked as possible by what she was about to do to him. He'd come home with a pretty little redhead, and had taken her immediately to his room for some nocturnal recreation.

Susannah sat, listening to the sounds of their passion which filtered right through the flimsy walls, not bothered in the least. One of the "side effects" of her killing was a fierce desire for sexual gratification afterwards, so she considered the grunts and groans that she was hearing from Jorge and his tart-du-jour to be nothing more than a bit of foreplay for her. Tim might be quiet and shy, but he was more than man enough to satisfy her needs when she came home from a kill, even if he was a bit awkward about it. He knew nothing of her activities, thinking that she was merely working on her art when she'd disappear for hours at a time.

Finally, sometime after midnight, the redhead giggled and kissed her way out the door and into her car. When the red taillights became tiny dots disappearing around the corner, Susannah's adrenalin kicked in, making her senses more keen, and her anticipation profound. She'd never taken drugs, partly because she could never imagine anything that might feel better than the rush she experienced when eyes went wide and realization dawned on the oppressors that they were no longer in control. She was. Polite, plain, ordinary Susannah had all the power – now *that* was a high.

She'd been inside Jorge's house a few times in preparation for the event. She'd learned the floor plan, as well as where he kept his cutlery. For the fine work, she'd use her own special instruments, but to just get the dirty deed of de-animation done, his would suffice. It wasn't very long before Susannah heard the soft rumbles of Jorge's snoring through his bedroom wall, and she was glad that he'd be nice and relaxed, it would make his terror upon waking all the more delicious. He couldn't charm his way out from under the blade of a knife.

Her hands were encased in thin, baby-soft leather gloves, and she used the key that she'd had made from Jorge's spare, which he kept under the doormat, to enter the dingy ranch-style home. She planned to melt the small brass key down to coat the tooth that she was going to extract from him, post-mortem. Soundlessly entering the home, Susannah headed straight for the kitchen, pulling open the drawer next to the stove and withdrawing a meat cleaver and a butcher knife, stifling a giggle over the thought that the knife would finally be used for its named purpose. She felt giddy with anticipation, but controlled her movements and her breathing for maximum effectiveness.

When Todd had passed, her mother had given his gym equipment to their chubby daughter, hoping that she might honor the memory of her father by finally getting in shape. Susannah actually did work out regularly, but only so that she could be more effective and precise in her morbid activities. Her adrenalin-fueled strength had allowed her to subdue grown men on more than one occasion, and she knew it wouldn't fail her tonight.

She crept down the hall to where Jorge snored, blissfully unaware that the relaxed breaths that he took were to be among his last. Susannah felt alive. Every nerve ending in her body was tingling with anticipation and she could practically hear the blood flowing through her veins. Her focus was singular – the house could burn down around her at this point, and she'd notice nothing but Jorge.

She stood beside his bed, watching his chest fall and rise with breath, excited by the pulse that she saw thumping in his neck. The light of the moon shone through the dirty window, illuminating her victim as though he'd been placed on a stage just for her entertainment. Her heart thudded within her. This was the most dangerous time, that time where all stood still and she observed her target, watching and waiting for them to swim upward to consciousness so that she could see the terror in their eyes just before she struck.

Jorge slept peacefully, while Susannah's need grew. When she could take it no longer, she put just the tip of the butcher knife to his neck to wake him, but still he slept on. She pressed the tip further, and he still did not wake. Frustrated that he wasn't responding like most of her victims did, she pressed the knife even further, until it pierced that beautiful skin just a bit, and at last, he startled awake, slapping at his neck as though he'd been bitten by a mosquito, and crying out when his hand came back with a wicked slice through the palm.

Dazed, he looked up at Susannah with an expression that was both pained and dumb, reminding her of a newly branded calf. He saw her hovering above him and was confused…until he saw the glint of moonlight on the meat cleaver in her left hand. Just when his eyes went wide, as the horrific reality of his plight dawned on him, she plunged the knife into his neck with all of her strength, reveling in the jet of blood that spurted from the wound when she withdrew it, enjoying the gurgling sounds he made as he tried to scream, and drawing an almost sexual satisfaction in the way his eyes begged her for mercy, for help, as he lay there twitching, bucking and dying. There it was. The control. He had just ceded control of his blood, his bodily functions, his life…to her, and she gloried in it.

She stood back and watched him struggle, but he couldn't gather the strength to even leave the bed, so that's where he would die, and she waited for him to get on with it. While she took great pleasure in watching the process, she had more work to do before she left the house, and she wanted to get a good night's sleep before her opening shift at the restaurant tomorrow.

She had slipped her feet into Jorge's shoes before

killing him, so that when she left, if the police found footprints, they'd be his, and she always made sure that her clothes were washable and unable to shed fibers and that her hair was tied tightly into synthetic cloth so that none escaped. Tim had shared a wealth of forensic information with her, unknowingly making her much safer.

When the last rush of breath left Jorge's lungs, Susannah flopped his hand onto the nightstand and in one quick motion, brought the meat cleaver down, severing it at the wrist, slipping it into a plastic bag that had been tucked into her belt. She then placed the cleaver in his other hand, wrapping his fingers around it to leave fingerprints, and left it where it fell, on the floor beside his bed. She could get skin leaves for the tree from the back of the hand, and if she wanted to play with texture a bit, she'd take one from the palm as well.

Susannah shuffled out the back door, to the little shed that was hidden in a tree-filled corner of the yard, where the moonlight couldn't penetrate. Stepping into the shed in Jorge's shoes, she sopped up the blood on her gloves with a rag used for wiping down the lawn mower, and peeled off her soiled clothes, placing them in a plastic bag that she'd stashed there a week ago, after Jorge had last mowed. She pulled a handful of disinfectant wipes from a container on a nearby shelf, and after dropping her gloves in the bag with the bloody clothing, she wiped down all the visible blood that had splashed her and threw the wipes on the floor of the shed. Dressing in clean clothing that she'd left in the shed along with the plastic bag, she listened for a moment before slipping back outside, carrying the evidence of her gleeful experience with her to dispose of later.

Susannah had an industrial sink in the building behind their house, where she butchered chickens, which would serve quite well as a washing machine for now. Tomorrow, after Tim left for work, she'd come home on her lunch hour and put the clothing in the actual washing machine. The gloves would burn in the fiercely hot oven that she used to fire an occasional clay pot, many of which were at least partially composed of the ashes of human and animal remains. They always sold well at county fairs.

Jorge's hand would be stashed in a freezer that she'd put in a secret room she'd discovered in the basement of the old cottage, until she could give it the attention it deserved. She couldn't wait to add Jorge's leaves to her tree. It had been a good night and a good kill, with plenty of time to savor the experience and plenty of souvenirs to include in her art. Now, she had business to take care of, and if Tim wasn't awake enough, she'd make sure that she made him ready to satisfy her. They'd keep all the lights out, just the way they liked it, and she'd shower after, in case she'd missed any blood spatter.

CHAPTER 10

"Susannah, I need to ask you a rather strange question," Tim remarked, poking a spoon in and out of his bowl of oatmeal to mix in the butter and brown sugar that swam on top.

Susannah's spoon stopped halfway to her mouth and she looked at him in an odd, rather panicked way.

"Okay…" she replied, setting the spoon down and staring at him.

"It's a bit…difficult for me to talk about," he sighed, putting his spoon down as well and staring at the table top.

Her eyes widened, then became shuttered, and she stared down at her cereal, deliberately nonchalant.

"Oh?" she said softly, trying to keep her voice from shaking.

"It's about…things you've done in the past, and I don't want to make you uncomfortable, but…" he trailed off.

"What?" her head snapped up and her eyes looked almost feverish.

Tim took a bite of his oatmeal and chewed slowly, avoiding her eyes. He swallowed, took a sip of his tea and stared at her.

"Okay, I'm just going to come out with it," he sighed, wondering why on earth she was looking at him like some kind of cornered animal. "A woman came by the office today, and she asked me a really strange question."

Susannah swallowed hard and seemed to pale a bit. "Really? About what?" she asked, her voice a much higher pitch than usual.

"She's been having issues with her veterinarian. She has a cat who's very ill, and the vet has just been giving her expensive supplements to keep the poor animal alive, and the cat is suffering," he explained, drawing a puzzled look from his wife.

"She came by the mortuary to tell you about her cat?"

"Yes, but that's not all," Tim fiddled with the handle of his spoon.

"Okaaaaay," Susannah seemed to be getting irritated, and wiped a light sheen of sweat from her upper lip.

"She wants to…needs to…put the cat out of its misery," he blew out a breath.

Susannah frowned deeply, thoroughly befuddled.

"Timothy, is there something in this story that will explain how this woman and her cat is any business of ours?" she asked sharply, adrenalin flowing. "Why on earth did she come to a mortuary to tell you about her cat? That makes no sense," she shook her head.

"Oh, right," he blinked at her. "Well, yes, it kind of does make sense. She's hoping that…she asked if…" he faltered.

"What? What did she ask? What did she want?" Susannah demanded, frustrated at her husband's reticence.

"She wants us to kill the cat," he said simply, a bit taken aback at the vehemence of his wife's questions.

For a brief moment, it appeared as though there was a glint of excitement in Susannah's eyes, but Tim was certain that he'd just imagined it. His wife was clearly just stressed out about something. Some time in her shop usually relaxed her – perhaps she'd sculpt something later.

"Oh," she replied, raising her eyebrows. "Why does she want us to do it?"

"She thought that I might have access to chemicals that would make it more humane," he shrugged, picking up his spoon again and digging into the congealing oatmeal.

"Do you?" Susannah was looking at him intently.

"I'm sure that I could come up with something, but I thought perhaps, since you grew up on a farm, you might know what to do."

"Well, if she's looking for a humane end to a family pet, anything that we used to do on the farm wouldn't be an acceptable option for her. We used things like sledge hammers and large knives and…" she began.

Tim held up a hand, looking slightly green. "Okay, I understand…please," he shook his head. "Don't worry, I'll figure something out."

"People get so attached to animals," his wife mused, returning to her breakfast. "It's fast and easy the way that we used to do it."

"Can we not discuss that during a meal?" Tim asked quietly. "Animals are innocent and it's barbaric what some humans do to them."

Susannah cocked her head to the side, chewing thoughtfully. "Okay," she nodded. "I never realized that you were such an animal lover."

Tim blinked at her from behind his thick lenses. "Animals don't hurt people. They eat and sleep and look beautiful and just try to live their lives. People should be more like that," he murmured, getting up from the table and taking his bowl with him.

Tim was a man of few words, and his wife stared at him in amazement after his assertions. He rarely spoke, and almost never showed emotion of any kind. His short monologue about animals was unusual to say the least.

"Should we get a pet?" she asked, trying not to shudder. Nurturing was definitely not her thing.

"No," he replied on his way to the kitchen.

He didn't turn around and she didn't say another word, finishing her oatmeal in silence, alone.

Shelby Myers came to the back door of the mortuary, carrying a blanketed bundle that looked like it might be a swaddled newborn, and quickly followed Tim down the his basement workroom.

"That's her?" he nodded at the bundle in her arms.

"Yes," was the tearful reply.

Shelby gently moved back a fold of the blanket, and Tim was regarded by two cloudy green eyes, peering out of a thin, furry face. Bootsie mewed weakly, and tears coursed down her owner's cheeks at the pitiful sound. Tim focused on the poor suffering animal, while her owner took deep shuddering breaths.

"This won't hurt her, will it?" she asked, clutching the suffering feline to her breast.

Tim shook his head. "No," he said quietly. "She'll fall into a deep sleep and never wake up."

He'd done his homework and had discovered how certain over the counter medications could be used to sedate and stop organ function in animals without pain or distress. He had syringes that were typically used for preparing different cavities in the body for burial, and he had filled one with a special cocktail that would ensure that the cat didn't suffer. She would fall into a deep sleep, and her organs would shut down without waking her.

"Okay," Shelby nodded shakily, her lower lip trembling. "What…what do I need to do?"

"I've prepared a place that should be comfortable for her," he gestured to a metal table where he'd made a nest of towels. "What would you like to do with the remains? I have a crematorium, if you'd like, I can…" he began, feeling distinctly uncomfortable broaching the subject while the sick cat wheezed from beneath her blanket.

"No," the grieving young woman shook her head. "There's no need for that. I'll take her home and bury her in the yard. There's a place beside my favorite rose bush," her chin quivered and she moved toward the nest of towels, placing the blanket and Bootsie down in the midst of it.

The cat made another attempt at a meow, sounding like the faintest cry of a gate creaking to and fro in the wind. Tim took a breath and looked away for a moment, as Shelby leaned down, stroking the thin fur that stretched across the clearly visible row of ribs along the cat's side, and giving her one last kiss on top of the head. She ran a finger under the furry chin one last time, and rested her hands on the cat's back, while Tim moved to the table, syringe in hand.

"Ready?"

She nodded, tears running freely down her cheeks.

"Bye-bye sweet baby kitty," she whispered, holding the fragile, sickly animal as best as she could while Tim found a vein.

Bootsie didn't even have the strength to react to the slight prick of the needle, and she was so weak that the medicine began working almost immediately. Her breathing slowed, the labored breaths becoming few and far between, until at last, maybe two minutes after injection, they ceased altogether.

"I don't feel her heartbeat anymore," Shelby put her head down on the cold metal table, her hands tenderly wrapped around the small, still body.

"I'm so sorry," Tim said, meaning it. He stepped back, allowing the young woman to grieve, and stood watching, arms folded.

After a few minutes, Shelby tried to take deep breaths to compose herself, but succeeded only in producing gasping hiccups and shudders. She wiped her eyes with the back of her hand, and gathered up the blanket, which now contained a limp, lifeless Bootsie.

"Thank you," she managed to choke out, on her way out the door. "Thank you for helping me."

Tim couldn't speak, so he merely nodded, feeling faintly nauseated. He closed the door behind Shelby and leaned against it, wracked with the sudden onset of bone-jarring chills. He had no way of knowing that when his wife saw the crying young woman leave, through their kitchen window next door…she smiled. The killer's husband had just taken his first life, and she was delighted.

CHAPTER 11

Arlen Bemis strode into Tim's basement workspace like he owned it, a toothpick clamped firmly between his teeth.

"Got a stiff for ya, Eckels. Need to come to the morgue to pick it up," he announced, as Tim stared at him, makeup sponge in hand. He had a funeral tomorrow, and was putting the finishing touches on Almira Motley, who had passed peacefully in her sleep.

"Okay," Tim nodded, going back to the task at hand.

"He's had an autopsy, and doesn't have any family that we can find, so it's gonna be a pine box and no funeral type thing. When you're done with whatever you do, let us know, and we'll take him to the county cemetery," the sheriff leaned back against a stainless steel sink.

"Okay," Tim repeated, not bothering to look up.

"And, one last thing, Eckels…"

Tim stopped applying foundation and regarded the sheriff with profound annoyance, trying not to sigh.

"There are some…unique things about this body that don't need to be public knowledge, you feel me?" Arlen raised a warning eyebrow.

Tim blinked at him blankly and pushed his glasses up his nose with the back of one gloved wrist. The sheriff looked irritated.

"His death is under investigation, but without family or friends around asking questions, it may not exactly be a high priority for us, and we don't need to have folks thinking that there's a dangerous killer on the loose. You get it that time?"

"Killer?"

"Look, just keep your mouth shut about any details regarding this stiff, got it?"

Tim nodded slowly. "Got it."

"Good. I think it's high time you figured out how things work around here, Eckels. You keep your mouth shut and your nose out of other folks' business and you'll do just fine."

Bemis took the toothpick out of his mouth and flicked it into the sink. Tim fought the urge to wrinkle his nose in disgust.

"Yes, sheriff," he gave the expected response.

"That's more like it, Eckels. Good man," half of Arlen Bemis's mouth turned upward in a mocking smile. "Hurry up and get down there to get him. He's taking up room in the fridge."

Tim stared after the sheriff as he swaggered arrogantly toward the stairs, then went back to working on Almira's youthful glow.

The county coroner, Leonard Kelson, a crusty old fart on the verge of retirement, looked like something from a vampire movie out of the sixties. His slicked-back, iron-gray hair revealed a widow's peak that would have rivaled any horror movie villain's, and his sagging jowls, pursed lips and neglected yellow teeth, made one wonder if he might just prefer his liver raw, with a nice dry wine. Timothy Eckels looked like a high-fashion model by comparison.

"Who the hell are you?" Kelson demanded, when Tim walked into his grey-walled office in the county building.

"I'm Timothy Eckels, I came to..." he began.

"Oh, you're here to pick up the body. Bout damn time," he groused. "What took you so friggin' long? Thought I'd have been able to get out of this godforsaken place hours ago," Lenny continued grumbling as he led Tim down into the bowels of the building, to the morgue.

The transfer from Lenny's cold storage to Tim's hearse was accomplished easily enough, and soon the mortician was on his way back to the comfort and solitude of his workroom. He brought the corpse to the basement on his own, wishing, not for the first time, that the elevator in the old Victorian had been automated, rather than hand-cranked. It wasn't that he was uncomfortable riding down with the body, far from it, it was the fact that so much valuable time was lost standing there, lowering the rickety car to the basement. He never used the elevator unless he was bringing in a body, so it wasn't an issue most of the time, but the very real possibility existed that he might one day get trapped in between floors with a rapidly warming corpse.

He laid out the body on the table to see what needed to be done to make it presentable. When the state paid for a burial, a mandatory one-hour viewing was required, just in case a friend or family member showed up out of the blue, and an open casket was preferred, if at all possible. The first obvious clue that this was no ordinary death, was a missing hand. The wound was clean, and looked as though it had been sliced through in one skillful swoop. The cause of death was apparently the slit carotid, which was also a clean, precise cut. That kind of precision was unusual in a homicide. Typically murderers slashed and hacked their way through skin, flesh and bone without any regard for technique. Further examination revealed that there was a patch of hair missing from the body, which looked like it had been pulled out post mortem. Tim's trained eye searched the body for other clues as to what may have happened, and he wondered what evidence had been gathered from the young man's corpse.

The mortician fixated on the wrist and how evenly the skin there had been cleaved. It reminded him of something that he couldn't quite put his finger on, but try as he might, nothing came to him when he tried to recall it, so he eventually gave up, examining the rest of the body. The fingernails on the remaining hand had been cut, and he gathered that the cranky coroner had done that, in hopes of finding some DNA evidence. Tim was more than disturbed that the sheriff didn't seem to be taking this particular homicide seriously, but had already more than figured out that there was nothing he could do about it. On that point, Arlen Bemis had been quite clear.

Because Almira Motley had been a well-respected member of the community, much like Tim's beloved Gram, he took his time making preparations for her funeral, and then went to work on Jorge Hernandez, finishing up after the dinner hour had long passed. His stomach growled, and when he trudged to the cozy cottage next door, he was surprised to see a light shining under the door to the basement. Susannah had seemed a bit stressed lately, so he assumed that she was working out her angst by crafting another sculpture. He never disturbed her when she was working in the basement. It was her realm, and he left her to it.

Tim was halfway through his dinner of leftover meatloaf and mashed potatoes when his wife came up the stairs from the basement, looking much happier than she had in a while. Her hands were shriveled slightly from wearing nitrile gloves for an extended period of time, so he knew that she'd been working on a project, which always seemed to lift her mood.

"Oh! Is it dinner time?" Susannah glanced at her watch surprised to see how late it had gotten. "I'm sorry, Timothy. I was working on a project and the time just got away from me."

"It's okay," he blinked at her, swallowing a bite of her delicious meatloaf. "I just got home, and this food looked so good that I heated it up. I didn't know that you hadn't eaten, or I would've made more."

"Don't you worry about it, Timmy," she kissed the top of his head in a rare show of affection on her way to the fridge. "I'll just fix some for myself and join you."

"That would be nice," he replied, staring at his plate.

He hated it when people called him Timmy. He had very few memories of his mother, but the one that stood out was her screaming "Timmy" at him when he was just a toddler, before she went away and his Gram came to rescue him.

Susannah heated up her food, a huge portion of it, and settled herself across the table from her husband. He watched as she tore into the food with delight, and something on the sleeve of her blouse caught his eye. He chewed his bite of meatloaf slowly, staring.

She washed a huge bite of mashed potatoes down with a gulp of ice cold milk and put down her glass, noticing her husband's gaze. She followed it and then looked back up at him.

"What?" she asked, sounding the tiniest bit defensive.

"There's a hair," he observed, trying not to grimace.

Stray hairs, particularly around food, were a source of discomfort for him, and this one was particularly offensive because it was short, black, and wavy. His wife's hair was long and blonde. Not only was there a hair near food, but it was a stranger's hair.

She looked down slowly and grasped the hair in between her thumb and forefinger, taking it to the trash.

"No big deal," she shrugged. "It's gone now," she dismissed her husband, who was still staring at her, not eating. "What?" she demanded, as he continued to blink at her from across the table.

"Your hair is blonde," he said quietly.

"What are you trying to say, Timothy?" her eyes narrowed.

Suddenly his appetite was gone, and he put down his fork, not only unable to eat another bite, but feeling the food that he had consumed rising in his throat a bit.

"That hair wasn't blonde."

Susannah glared at him, reminding him somehow of his mother. "Are you accusing me of something, Timothy?" she asked, teeth clenched, nostrils flaring.

"I...I don't...it's just," he faltered, feeling oddly helpless in the face of her anger.

"Well, are you?" she demanded, slamming her fork down on the table, causing him to wince. "How dare you, Timothy Eckels?" she challenged, eyes spitting fire.

In that moment, the universe came into sharp focus for Tim. He'd been treated like this before, the cold shudders that he felt in his soul brought back memories that he didn't know he had. Time slowed down, and he felt quite certain that he could feel the blood thrumming through his veins. The cold look on her face, the hatred in her eyes, he'd been in this place before, and he refused to go back.

"There's no need for shouting," he said, suddenly cold and calm. "It caught my attention because it wasn't yours and it wasn't mine and I wondered whose it might be. Your reaction makes me wonder if you have something that you'd like to tell me though," he said quietly, his eyes chips of ice.

Susannah stared at him. She'd always wondered if her mild-mannered, terribly introverted husband actually had a backbone, and his tone just then had shown that he did. In spades.

"I have nothing to say to you," she growled, getting up from the table. She tossed her plate in the sink so hard that it shattered on impact.

"I'm not cleaning that up," Tim remarked, picking up his fork, determined to enjoy the rest of his meal.

Susannah shot him another glare and headed for the door. "It had better be cleaned up by the time I get back," she said on her way out.

"Don't hold your breath," Tim commented lightly as the door slammed shut.

Once she was gone, he no longer had to keep up the pretense of being hungry, so he dropped his fork onto his plate in disgust, the utensil making a dull thud when it landed in the mashed potatoes. He stood up, took his plate to the sink and tossed it in on top of Susannah's. It clattered, suffering a chip on the rim, and he looked at it with grim satisfaction. He'd avoided relationships his entire life because he generally found his fellow humans to be a dramatic, irrational lot, and his interaction with his wife had just underscored that belief. What had he gotten himself into?

CHAPTER 12

This was the part that Timothy Eckels hated about his job. His neck chafed under the understated blue and gray patterned tie that he wore with his standard charcoal-colored mortician costume. It was a viewing day, and there was a chance, despite the fact that this particular victim had been alone in the world, that someone might come in to pay their last respects, and he'd have to interact with them. The tears, the concerned faces, the hysteria – Tim was supremely uncomfortable with all of it - but was professionally obligated to play the part of the caring overseer of all things funerary. A buzzer sounded, indicating that the front door had opened, and Tim sighed, taking one last look in the mirror to check that no hair was out of place before trudging up to greet the guests of the dead.

Tim entered the viewing parlor that featured hunter-green plush carpet with matching drapes, and digni-fied burgundy wallpaper with touches of gold. He'd covered the rudimentary pine casket in black satin, giving the simple box a more upscale look. Even the indigent dead deserved to be presented with excel-lence, and this handsome corpse was showcased to the best of Tim's abilities. The bottom half of the casket was closed, and a black satin sheet was draped over the body up to the elbow so that Jorge's hands, or lack thereof, didn't show. The precise laceration in his neck was hidden by a snow white shirt collar, making his olive skin look tanned and healthy. Tim was truly an artist, and regarded each body as a blank canvas that had a story to tell.

A large, imposing man was standing near the casket, his face looking more puzzled than sad.

"I don't get it," the man said, shaking his head.

"I'm sorry for your loss," Tim said, pulling out the standard phrase, hands clasped in front of him.

"We weren't close, honestly. We worked together at Le Chateau. I was kind of his boss."

"My wife works at Le Chateau," Tim offered, feeling oddly unnerved.

"I'm Andre Guillaume, Head Chef," Andre offered his hand and Tim shook it. "Who's your wife?"

"Susannah Eckels. I'm Tim. She didn't mention that one of her co-workers had died."

Andre gave him a strange half-smile.

"Well, Jorge wasn't exactly her favorite person," Andre shrugged. "Everyone else on the planet, especially women, seemed to like him, but he seemed to just rub Susannah the wrong way."

"Oh?"

"Well, as I'm sure you know, your wife is a bit of a perfectionist, and Jorge was somewhat haphazard in his kitchen habits."

Tim nodded. "Yes, she wouldn't have had much patience for that," he agreed.

"I guess it doesn't matter now, though," Andre said ruefully.

"I suppose not," the mortician said, at a loss for words.

"You did a good job. He looks like he's just sleeping."

"Thank you."

"How did he die anyway? No one seems to know anything. I mean, Jorge seemed like a healthy guy…"

"I…uh…I'm not certain that I know…" Tim was interrupted by the arrival of his wife.

"Hello Andre," she said quietly, approaching the casket. She and Tim hadn't spoken since their disagreement the night before.

"Susannah," the chef nodded.

She glanced at the casket, her face expressionless, then looked at her boss.

"Do we have a new prep cook yet?" she asked gravely.

Both men just blinked at her.

"Good god, Susannah, Jorge just died," Andre frowned.

She nodded pensively. "Right, you haven't had time to interview yet, I understand."

She peered into the casket one last time, staring at the

spot that Tim had artfully covered, where Jorge's hair had been pulled out. "Goodbye, Jorge," she said mechanically, then turned and left the parlor, with her husband and boss staring after her.

"People grieve in their own way," Tim offered lamely, not looking at Andre.

"Yeah," the chef grunted. "Nice to meet you, Tim. I'm heading out."

"Thanks for stopping by," the mortician replied, his mind elsewhere.

Susannah only came over to the mortuary when he specifically asked her to do something because he was going to be busy with a large funeral or something. The fact that she had come over of her own accord, while still not talking to her husband, was strange to say the least. Tim wondered if perhaps his wife had more emotional capacity than he did, and had just come to say goodbye to a co-worker. His heart softened a bit at the thought, and he made plans to talk things out with her after Jorge's viewing was over.

"Alright, Eckels, wrap it up, it's been an hour,"

Sheriff Arlen Bemis drawled, ambling into the viewing parlor.

"Umm...no, Sheriff, it hasn't. It's only been twenty minutes," Tim tapped his watch.

"Look here, Dr. Frankenstein, I don't care if it's been twenty seconds, we got a crew out at the cemetery waitin' to put this boy in the ground, and they get paid by the hour, so you need to load him up and take him over, understand?"

"But the law says that..." he began, puzzled as to why the sheriff was in such a hurry.

Bemis interrupted him, stepping up and thrusting his nose squarely into the mortician's personal space bubble.

"In case you ain't figured it out yet, I *am* the law around here, and I say it's time to go, so get moving and get this stiff outta here," he ordered.

Tim stared at him, confounded.

"I...okay," he sighed, not wanting to deal with any more hostility from the sheriff.

Jorge Hernandez had been just another body, but

there was something about his death that stuck in Tim's craw. Something was wrong, perhaps murderously wrong, and he just couldn't put his finger on it.

"I just dropped your co-worker off at the county cemetery," Tim said quietly when he came into the living room where Susannah was watching television.

"Andre?" she raised an eyebrow at him.

"No. Jorge. You didn't tell me that one of your co-workers had died...I could've...I don't know... hugged you or something," he glanced away, embarrassed.

"What makes you think that I need a hug?" she asked, gazing down at the floor.

"I just...I didn't know if you were...maybe, sad...or something."

"I didn't really know him."

"Okay," Tim stood there awkwardly, hands in his pockets. "Do you want to go out to dinner or something?" he offered, not knowing how to comfort his wife when she didn't seem to need comforting.

She looked at her husband as though weighing her options, and he was somewhat afraid of what she might say, though he didn't know why. Seeming to come to a decision, her expression softened a bit.

"Can we just get take-out instead? There's a movie coming on tonight that I want to watch. It's about a girl with multiple personalities."

"Okay, that sounds interesting," he nodded, relieved that their storm had passed. "Pizza or Chinese?"

"Pizza, with extra garlic."

"Do you want to come with me to pick it up?" he offered.

"No, you go ahead," she waved him off. "I have some things to take care of around here."

CHAPTER 13

Susannah had seriously considered killing her husband after he confronted her about the hair on her blouse. She'd gotten careless, but fully realized that a temper tantrum which snuffed out the life of her mild-mannered mate would be ill-advised. Married people are normal people. Married people aren't looked upon as potential perpetrators of mayhem and murder. Married people get along, and if she eliminated Timothy, she'd be just another single and suspicious female.

Andre had hired a plump, young Italian woman, Rosa Fenetti, to replace Jorge, and, as far as Susannah could tell, she and the new girl were going to get along just fine. While the young woman was a bit melodramatic, and far too talkative, her precise use of knives and measurement devices was commendable. A week after Rosa had started at Le Chateau, Susannah arrived at work to find the young woman in tears in the break room.

"Onions?" she asked, stifling her impatience. Susannah had no tolerance for weakness, particularly when it manifested in tears.

Rosa jumped, not having heard her coworker come in, and hurriedly wiped her eyes.

"No," she shook her head, not making eye contact.

"Cut yourself?" Susannah tried again, forcing herself to sound at least marginally concerned.

She hadn't seen any blood on the new girl, which unfortunately meant that Rosa was most likely blubbering about some wretched emotional thing that she didn't want to deal with, and she'd be more than upset if it threw her prep schedule off.

"No...it's my...Veektor," she said, choking a bit on the name, and pressing a sodden tissue under her eyes.

"Victor? Is that your boyfriend or something?" It took

a supreme amount of effort for Susannah to refrain from sighing.

Rosa shook her head again.

"No. Veektor…is my baby," her face twitched with sorrow.

"Oh, your son?"

"No, he's my little doggie. I love him so much and he's very seeck," she replied, her shoulders hitching.

"Your dog," Susannah's voice was flat and it took everything within her not to roll her eyes.

Rosa nodded.

"The vet say that he will get better with the supplements, but I been giving them to heem for two weeks, and still he gets worse. He looks up at me with the sad eyes, and I just can't take eet no more."

A gleam appeared briefly in Susannah's eyes, and she sat down next to her coworker, taking the distraught young woman's hand.

"I hate to ask such an awful question," she began, quietly. "But, have you thought about…putting poor little Victor out of his misery. Sometimes it's the best thing that you can do," she patted the olive-skinned young hand in her palm, admiring the color.

"That's just the theeng," Rosa exclaimed. "I tell the vet that my Veektor, he need to be put down, even though I don't want heem to go away, and he say no. He say the supplements, they will work in time, but they don't, and I don't know what to do. My Veektor, he suffering," she sobbed.

"I may be able to help you," Susannah soothed, biting the inside of her cheek to keep from smiling at her plan.

"But Timmy, this poor young woman is suffering, and so is her dog. What is she supposed to do?" Susannah pleaded, grabbing Tim's hand as they sat side by side on the couch.

"What your coworker does with her sick dog is none of my business, nor any of yours," he stared at her, unyielding, from behind his thick glasses.

"It does affect me. I have to see that sad face day after day, and when she doesn't perform well because she's upset, it directly affects my job," she insisted.

"Then perhaps you should take up her performance issues with your boss," he suggested, blinking at her.

"That's your answer? Just forget about the feelings of this poor woman, and the suffering of an innocent animal, and tell her boss, so that she might get fired because she's too distraught to work properly? What kind of human are you?"

"This isn't about me," Tim sighed, withdrawing his hand and turning off the television.

"Oh, but it is. You know how to stop this dog from suffering, you know how to ease this woman's pain, and yet you refuse. This is entirely about you," Susannah drew away from her husband, shaking her head in disbelief, her show of emotion baffling him.

"Why do you care so much?" he asked.

"Because I would like to think that if it were me in that situation, that some kind, compassionate soul would be willing to help me out, that's why," Susannah replied, standing, in a huff. "I'm going to bed, and I'll probably be gone before you leave in the morning. I have an early shift tomorrow," she shot him one last accusing look before heading down the hall toward the bedroom.

She heard a sigh, then heard the creak of the couch springs as Tim stood to follow her.

"Susannah, wait…" he called out, resignation coloring his tone.

She was able to wipe the smug grin from her face before he caught up with her in the hall to tell her that he'd help Rosa Fenetti with her dog, but that it would absolutely be the last time that he did anything like that. After he'd made his promise, she led him by the hand to the bedroom, and gave him a little something special to help him sleep. As he snored beside her, she stifled a giggle. Wouldn't it be so much fun to start her mild-mannered mortician husband down the path of becoming a cold-blooded killer? She'd finally have someone with whom she could swap stories and be fully herself. She'd be free to talk about the activities that gave her the highest of highs. If Timmy was a murderer, they'd have so much more in common. Susannah Eckels began making plans in her head, and fell asleep with a smile on her face.

CHAPTER 14

"Have you seen this dog?" Sheriff Arlen Bemis thrust a photo of Rosa Fenetti's dog, Victor, under Timothy Eckels' nose as he was closing up the mortuary after a long day of body prep.

Tim stood, blinking at the sheriff, not letting his anxiety show.

"I haven't left the mortuary today, how on earth could I have seen that dog?" he asked, irritated.

"I didn't ask you if you saw him today, I asked you if you've seen him," Bemis persisted, chomping on his omnipresent toothpick.

"No, I don't get out much, and I don't generally pay

attention to dogs when I'm out and about. I'm allergic," Tim shrugged.

"Uh-huh," the sheriff's eyes narrowed suspiciously. "Then why is it that Mrs. Truman, from across the street, seems to recall having seen this dog entering your mortuary?"

"She drinks."

"Boy, you trying to tell me that an upstanding member of this community is seeing things because she has a drinking problem?" the sheriff tapped the end of Tim's nose with the photo, standing very close.

"Your words, not mine, Sheriff," the mortician gazed back at him impassively.

"Where's this dog now?" Bemis demanded, looming over Tim.

"How should I know? Wouldn't that be a good question to ask his owner?"

"And who might that be?" the sheriff moved closer, trying to trip Tim up.

"I have no idea, but I would assume that it's whomever you got that picture from."

"You gettin' smart with me, boy?" Bemis growled.

Tim stared back at the frustrated sheriff, somehow knowing that his best course of action was to remain silent.

"I'm watching you," the sheriff said, finally backing off and tucking the photo of the dog back into his shirt pocket. "You better watch your step. If you commit a crime in my county, I'm gonna bust you so hard, you ain't never gonna see the light of day, you got it?"

"Okay," Tim blinked at him, maintaining his composure until the sheriff was pulling out of the parking lot.

The mortician took a deep breath and let it out slowly, knowing that the ashes of Rosa's Lhasa Apso, Victor, would be coming out of the oven soon, to be placed in a small porcelain jar, which Rosa had inherited from her grandmother.

"You can't bring me anymore people who have sick animals," Tim told Susannah at dinner. "The sheriff came by today, asking lots of questions, and he had a picture of Rosa's dog."

"Wow, that old country boy picked up a trail? I wouldn't think he'd be able to find his way out of a paper bag," she snickered, twirling strands of spaghetti around her fork.

"This isn't a joking matter, Susannah," Timothy stared at her.

"I'm sorry, you're right," she nodded, sobering.

"Has Rosa been happier?"

"Much. She's doing a great job with prep," his wife stuffed a forkload of pasta into her mouth. She'd made the sauce from scratch and it was perfect.

"That's good."

They finished the rest of their meal in relative silence, and watched television until it was time for bed.

"I'm telling you, Arlen, there have been two of my patients who have died recently, and there was nothing wrong with them that my supplements couldn't fix," Bradley Dobbins, the town veterinarian protested.

The sheriff had come to tell him that he'd questioned Timothy Eckels, and believed that the mortician was telling the truth.

"I mean, who trusts morticians anyway? They're the creepiest people on the planet, the handsome forty-something vet declared.

"Now look, Dobbins, you know as well as I do that Julia Truman isn't exactly what most folks would call a reliable source," the sheriff raised an eyebrow.

"Come on, Arlen...Julia may tip the bottle on occasion, but she's a hard-core animal lover. She's got her Muffy at my office at least once a week to make sure that her cat is the healthiest cat in town."

The sheriff, being a man who didn't particularly see the appeal of living with animals in the home, regarded the vet with vague distaste. "And that's entirely normal," he snorted.

"Look, she's not out to get the mortician, she's just concerned about animals, and if my patients are being exterminated by this man, he should be prosecuted, that's all I'm saying," Bradley lifted his hands, palms up, in appeal.

"I think it's a pretty big leap to go from a drunk woman's report of seeing a dog going into the mortuary to accusing a man of killing off your patients."

"We don't know that she was drunk," Dobbins grumbled.

"I'll keep an eye on him. He's a bit off, but he doesn't strike me as an animal killer," the sheriff shrugged.

"I hope you're right...cuz it seems to me that it'd be awfully embarrassing for you if something like that was happening right under your nose and you did nothing about it."

The sheriff did his best not to glare at the vet, who was quite well-regarded in town.

"You have a good day, Dobbins," he muttered, stalking away before he lost his temper.

"Timmy, do you think of what you do with the bodies

as art?" Susannah asked, after they'd settled in under the covers.

"It seems to me to be more of a science. There are procedures involved," he murmured sleepily, the conversation making him a bit uneasy.

"Well, yes, but...when you make people look like they're still healthy and alive, don't you think that requires a bit of artistry?" she persisted.

"I suppose," he replied, just wanting the conversation to end so that he could go to sleep.

"Does it give you satisfaction to see the deceased looking so good?"

"Sure."

"Wouldn't you like to feel that way more often?" she asked, causing Tim's eyes to snap open in the darkness.

"What do you mean? I can only work with whatever bodies are available," the mortician commented, nervous about where this conversation might be going.

"Well, you know how you helped Rosa, and that

Shelby girl...what if you could..." she began, reaching for him in the darkness.

He brushed her hand away, appalled.

"Absolutely not. Work my craft on animals? Particularly animals that didn't die of natural causes? I think not," he huffed, turning away from her and pulling the covers up around his neck.

"I mean...I would think that skin is skin, eyes are eyes, faces are faces...does it really matter whether they're human or animal? What if the owners want you to preserve their pet so that they can remember them exactly as they were? You could make them happy..." Susannah murmured, running a hand up Tim's back.

He didn't bother to even try to repress the shudder that rippled through him, and didn't dignify her question with a response. She sighed and took her hand away.

"Just think about it, Timmy. You might find it fun."

"Don't call me Timmy," he whispered under his breath, wide awake.

CHAPTER 15

"You've outdone yourself this time," Andre praised Susannah.

He'd given his Assistant Chef the freedom to create a new dish, and had featured it as a special. Not only were the patrons giving the dish rave reviews, but Andre himself had proclaimed that it was outstanding and innovative.

"Thanks," shy Susannah blushed, looking down. She was unaccustomed to praise, and the warm feelings that his word sent rushing through her made her more than a bit uncomfortable…but in a good way.

"I think we may start having you create a new dish once a week. Would you like that?"

Susannah raised her head and stared at him in disbelief.

"I...I would love that," she stammered. Creating new dishes was another art form for her, and to be recognized for her work was overwhelming.

Andre nodded.

"Great, we'll make it happen, and we'll see about getting you a raise to go along with it, how does that sound?" he grinned.

"That works," she nodded, wide-eyed.

"Susannah," Kelcie, the floor manager came rushing into the kitchen, her eyes bright. "There's a customer who would like to speak with you."

Susannah's heart sped up, and her eyes narrowed. "Why?"

Kelcie giggled. "It's a positive thing, don't worry. Just c'mon," she hooked her arm through Susannah's, practically dragging her toward the dining room.

Sensing Susannah's resistance, Andre encouraged her, calling out, "Go ahead, he probably wants to tell you how amazing you are."

Susannah wasn't the least bit comfortable with the thought of having to interact with a customer, but she didn't see that she had much choice in the matter. She briefly considered whether or not Kelcie's thin skin would make attractive leaves, but dismissed the thought. Kelcie was nice, just a young, exuberant puppy who meant well, but was clumsy in her interactions.

"This is our very talented Assistant Chef, who created your dinner," Kelcie pushed Susannah toward a man who sat beaming at her, then scurried off to check on another table.

"It's a pleasure to meet the artist behind the dish," the man said, sticking out his hand for her to shake. "I'm Brad Dobbins," he introduced himself. "And I am very much enjoying my dinner, thanks to you."

"Susannah. You're welcome," she said, trying to form a polite smile, despite her discomfort.

"You're the new undertaker's wife, right? You two are new in town?"

"Yes, that's right," she replied, feeling uneasy all of the sudden.

"Your work is very precise. Your husband must appreciate that about you. I would imagine you'd have incredible knife skills in your line of work. Does he as well?" the veterinarian asked casually, sipping his wine, and holding her gaze over the rim of his glass.

"Do you dine alone often?" Susannah asked, ignoring the inflammatory question, a deadly calm flooding through her.

"Divorced," he replied with a rueful smile, showing her his empty ring finger.

"Pity."

"It's for the best. I've found that having only myself for company is better than having bad company," he smiled, his gaze traveling up and down her body.

"Kids?"

"They're with her most of the time," he shrugged. "I get holidays and the occasional weekend."

Susannah nodded. That would make her job easier.

"Well, I'm glad you're enjoying your food. Have a

good rest of the evening," she said, turning away from the table.

"Susannah," he caught her hand as she turned and held it briefly before releasing it, causing waves of revulsion to churn in her stomach. "I'd like to meet your husband sometime. You know, one local businessman to another."

"What is your line of work?" she asked coolly.

"I'm the veterinarian here in town."

Realization dawned on her at that moment, and if she hadn't already been plotting his death, that admission would've clinched the deal.

"I see. You can find him at the mortuary if you'd like to introduce yourself," she replied, her brain spinning with need…and ideas.

"Thanks, I'll take you up on that," he smiled affably, having not an inkling that the woman in front of him would be personally escorting him from this world to the next.

"May I help you?" Tim asked the man who wandered into the mortuary, interrupting his work on a recent victim of an automobile accident.

"Are you Timothy?"

"I am."

"Brad Dobbins," the man introduced himself. "I ran into your wife the other day at Le Chateau, and it reminded me that I hadn't stopped by yet to welcome you to Pellman."

"Oh, thanks," Tim blinked at him after shaking his hand.

"I'm the local veterinarian, but you probably knew that," Dobbins grinned smugly.

"Uh, no. I don't have pets."

"Well, if you're looking for one, I have a few up for adoption at the clinic," the vet wandered around the mortuary, hands in his pockets, his eyes darting this way and that, as though he were looking for something.

"We don't have time for pets," Tim shrugged.

"Do you not like animals?" Brad peered at him.

"I think animals are beautiful and innocent."

Dobbins nodded. "Yes they are. Sometimes they're the only family members that folks have."

The vet moved casually toward the stairs, where the preparation rooms were located.

"What's down here?" he asked, stepping onto the first step.

"That's my work area," Tim replied. "You can't go down there."

"Really? I'm curious as to what a mortuary work area looks like. You can't give me a tour?"

Tim shook his head, wishing the obnoxious man would go away.

"No, I'm sorry, I'm right in the middle of something. You can call later this week to make an appointment if you'd like a tour. If I'm not too busy, I could show you around," he offered, hoping to get rid of his unwanted guest.

"I can just go through myself and take a look if it'd be easier for you. I won't touch anything," Dobbins persisted.

"Sorry, not possible. Now, if you'll excuse me, I have some unfinished work to attend to," Tim stared him down.

Dobbins pursed his lips and raised an eyebrow at the mortician.

"Okay, I get it," he conceded, holding up his hands in a conciliatory gesture. "No harm, no foul. Quick question though…have you ever had anybody come back on you?"

"What?" Tim blinked at the vet.

"You know…has there ever been someone who seemed to be dead, but later you found out that they weren't? I've heard that stuff like that happens sometimes."

"No," Tim said flatly. He was very serious about his profession and didn't appreciate it when strangers asked irreverent questions.

"How do you prevent that?"

"I make certain that the deceased is actually deceased. Won't you excuse me?" Tim had had enough, and led Bradley Dobbins to the door.

"Nice chatting with you, Tim," he shook the mortician's hand again.

"Likewise," was the toneless reply.

"Your wife's cooking is amazing…maybe we can all do dinner sometime?"

"We'll get back to you," Tim smiled thinly, saying whatever he needed to make the vet go away.

"Great, I'll be in touch."

CHAPTER 16

When Susannah arrived at Le Chateau, she found Andre having a conversation with the sheriff in his office. She couldn't hear what was being said, but saw the grim look on the Head Chef's face, and saw him shaking his head vehemently at times. When the sheriff emerged a short time later, heading immediately for the exit, the world-renowned chef muttered expletives to himself in French, picked up a meat cleaver, and began vigorously disassembling fresh ducks that had just been delivered.

"Everything okay?" Susannah asked, not because she cared about the chef's emotional state, but because she wanted to know what the conversation with the sheriff had been about. Given her somewhat unusual hobbies, she had an inherent mistrust of those in authority.

Andre spat out another French word that sounded like it must've been a curse.

"That peasant comes in here asking questions about my food, as if I'd use anything but the finest ingredients. It's an insult," the chef fumed.

"Did someone complain? Why would the sheriff care?"

"He was insinuating that I might be killing local animals for my dishes."

"He said that?" Susannah's heartbeat sped up a bit.

"No. He implied it. Same difference," Andre growled.

"But, we do use locally sourced meats and fish."

"Yes, but not cats and dogs, and we don't do the killing ourselves."

"Well, no. That would be...gross," she busied herself with tying on her apron and snapping on her gloves.

"Peasant," Andre proclaimed, bringing the meat

cleaver down and severing the neck of the duck in a manner that had Susannah's pulse racing with need.

The sheriff and the vet were becoming problems. She'd have to be very careful in the elimination of one or both of them, since they were both high-profile figures in the community. It was time for a bit of reconnaissance.

Sometimes before taking a life, Susannah would spend time getting to "know" her intended victim by roaming about their home, touching certain objects with her gloved hands, even standing over them, breathing in their breath while they slept. She intended to get to know the vet, his habits, his preferences, his peculiarities, so that when she finally drained the lifeblood from him, she'd be able to do it in a manner that would have a profound impact upon him in the moments before his death. She loved the element of surprise, and she loved seeing the horror in the eyes of those who were accustomed to being in control.

Bradley Dobbins shouldn't have spoken to her the way that he did, as though he were in control. He shouldn't have asked to speak with her at work, he shouldn't have grabbed her hand, touching her without permission, and he definitely shouldn't have dared to invade Tim's safe space, the mortuary, even though she had told him that he could. He was willing his presence into their lives, and she wouldn't put up with that. Susannah and her husband needed their privacy, and Bradley was trying to invade their personal bubbles, which was entirely unacceptable.

After a light dinner, Tim had gone to the mortuary to preside over a funeral, expecting to be gone all evening. The family of the deceased was large, and a caterer had been employed for the viewing, which meant that he'd have to work diligently to usher the crowd out of the understated interior of the funeral home before things got out of hand. It was an evening that he viewed with much trepidation, which worked out wonderfully for Susannah.

She'd been itching to get over to the veterinarian's home so that she could begin her observation of his habits and lifestyle, and Tim's evening at the mortuary would give her just the opportunity that she needed. Dressing in her black, fiber-free clothing, she secured her hair, donned her gloves, and headed for the exclusive side of Pellman, where she'd have to work her way around neighborhood gates, sensitive alarm systems, and nosy night watchmen. At least the designer dogs that these folks tended to have shouldn't pose much of a threat.

The air was getting cooler. Soon the turning of the season would pose its own challenges. Footprints were easy to see in frost-covered grass, crouching in bushes became much more of an ordeal when temperatures dropped, and disposing of bodies effectively sometimes became an issue. Despite the fact that heat made Susannah uncomfortable, summertime certainly had its advantages.

Bradley Dobbins had a blue and white alarm system sign in his yard, snugged into a picture perfect mound of mulch, but when she looked for the telltale signs of an actual system in the form of cameras, wires on windows and sensors around the property, there were none. It had been her experience in many of the uptight, exclusive neighborhoods, that the security, just like the McMansions and Swedish "build it yourself" furniture, was just for show. There were typically several homes which had the signs, but only a handful of them actually employed the services.

Susannah slipped into the side yard, reaching through

the bars of the wrought-iron gate that was set into the brick wall surrounding the property, to let herself into the back yard. It never failed to astonish her that folks would go to the trouble of putting up a brick wall, then install a gate that even the simplest of intruders could thwart. She closed the gate silently behind her, thankful that she'd brought a small canister of lubricant, with which she had sprayed the hinges before attempting to open it. She'd found very few issues in life that couldn't be addressed with either an application of lubricant or duct tape, depending upon the circumstances.

There was a large swimming pool in the back yard, and fortunately, the lights around it had already been turned off for the evening. Between the pool and the house was a large deck, and behind the French doors off of the deck was a spacious kitchen, where Bradley Dobbins was currently reaching into a stainless steel state-of-the-art refrigerator for a beer. Susannah smirked. With the long hours that the vet worked, she guessed that within a few minutes of finishing his beer in front of the television, Brad would be fast asleep. After watching him settle into his overstuffed leather couch, in a living room lit only by the television, she crept around the back of the house, to get an idea of the layout. While large, the home was quite simply designed, which would make getting in, memorizing it, and getting out again, a snap. She had wanted to just get a feel for the place tonight, and come back another time, when Dobbins wasn't home, to do some exploring, but the thought of slipping through the dark shadows of his home while he dozed on the couch was far too compelling, and after she did as much external exploration as she could, she waited until she saw his head drop to the side and stay there before trying window latches.

Luck was with her, she found a window on the side of the kitchen unlatched. Slipping the screen off, she pulled the casement window toward her just enough so that she could slip inside. There was a vintage aluminum dinette set below the window that made her resort to a series of contortions that would allow her to avoid the obstacle, but she managed, thanks to years of physical conditioning, and dropped to her feet as soundlessly as the cat who entered the room and gazed at her curiously while she went about her business.

First things first, she went through all of the kitchen drawers, assessing the collection of blades that might be put into use, and found a handful of adequate possibilities, then she went in search of two things: a suitable location for the main event, and a bag which might contain emergency veterinary tools. Who knew what lovely possibilities might lie in such a thing? A smile danced about her lips at the thought.

Bradley Dobbins' fat grey tabby followed Susannah around, as she moved quietly from room to room, familiarizing herself with the house and sorting through all sorts of delicious scenarios in her mind. The cat would meow every once in a while, and Susannah absently scratched its ears when it twined around her ankles as she knelt beside the vet's bed, going through the drawer in his nightstand. She withdrew a handgun, tucking it into her waistband, not so that she could use it, but merely as a precaution, so that he couldn't use it, in the unlikely event that he woke and found her in his house.

Bradley seemed to enjoy the pleasure of his own company, which was evident when she found a stack of explicit magazines, a bottle of lotion and a box of tissues in the next drawer down. Taking out one of the magazines, she laid it on the bed and strategically squirted a few blobs of lotion onto the centerfold, then pushed the drawer mostly shut and moved on to the closet. She noticed a fair number of pairs of sandals in his walk-in closet, flip-flops, both cloth and leather, climbing and hiking sandals, and even an old, ratty pair of rubber shower shoes. She wondered if he had attractive feet. Most folks didn't, so if this guy had model feet, she might want to take her souvenirs from there.

Susannah heard a snort from the living room which might indicate that the vet had snored himself awake. She crouched low and moved back into the darkened hall which led to the living room, holding her breath, listening. She could kill him now if it came to that, but she really preferred to do more planning first, since he was rather well-known. Her heart raced, not in fear, but in anticipation of what she would do to this man who had no idea of how fragile and vulnerable he really was.

When the low rumble of his slumber resumed, she made her way back out of the kitchen, using the French doors this time, which she left unlocked and partially open, just to start building a sense of fear and paranoia within the vet. She moved quickly to the gate, keeping watch for any figures in windows of surrounding houses, and let herself out. She'd no sooner closed the gate when a voice came from the shadows, startling her.

"Hey! You there!" a rather frail-looking elderly man came running toward her, in a slow, hitching fashion.

Susannah was still in the shadows, so she was certain that he couldn't see her face, and her hair was hidden underneath its wrap, so identifying her would be nearly impossible. She made a split-second decision, lunging at the old man and tackling him before he knew what hit him. Knocking him out with one punch, before he ever even caught a glimpse of her, she rose to her feet and bolted, taking a darkly shadowed route through side yards and common areas, until she was free from the enclave of the over-privileged. Tim was still busy at the mortuary when she returned, no doubt cleaning up after the boisterous wake, so she took a long, hot bath, and went to bed. The would-be assassin was sound asleep when her husband slipped under the covers beside her.

CHAPTER 17

Bradley Dobbins awoke with a start, his living room awash in revolving red and blue lights. A knock sounded at his door and he opened it to find Pellman's finest, Sheriff Arlen Bemis, looking grim.

"Arlen? What's going on?" the veterinarian tried to rub the sleepiness from his eyes.

"Your neighbor, Mr. Crothers, got attacked in your yard."

"What? Attacked? By whom? And why?" Dobbins blinked blearily, trying to process the shocking information.

"That's what I'm here to find out. You have any

company this evening?" he asked, staring pointedly at the empty beer bottle in Brad's hand.

"No. I came home from a very long day, had a beer in front of the TV and fell asleep. Did Crothers see the guy?"

Bemis shook his head.

"Nope, just saw your gate moving and a shadow coming out. Whoever it was tackled him and knocked him out cold. Old guy called 911 as soon as he came to. You got anything missing around here?" the sheriff asked, glancing past the vet, into the house.

"I have no idea. Like I said, I just now woke up, I think because of the lights."

"I'm gonna be out here for a while. I've got some forensics geeks coming out to search the attack site. Take a look around and come get me if you find anything peculiar," Bemis directed, poking a fresh toothpick between his teeth and chomping down on it.

"Okay, yeah," Dobbins ran a hand through his hair and started flipping on lights.

When he came to the kitchen, he paused, seeing the French doors open a few inches. To his right a breeze ruffled the curtain above the dinette, and he noticed that the screen was missing and the window was open. Feeling the hairs on the back of his neck raise just a bit, he scanned the kitchen, looking for other clues, and saw that his oversized utensil drawer hadn't closed completely. He felt a light touch on his ankle and nearly jumped out of his skin.

"Dammit Oscar," he hissed at the cat, closing his eyes for a moment and taking a deep breath.

The giant tabby looked balefully up at him and uttered a nearly silent meow.

"You could've come and woken me up," the vet muttered illogically at the unfazed feline, who sank down on his haunches and began washing his face with his paw.

"Find anything?" Arlen Bemis called from the foyer.

"In here…I think someone was in my kitchen," Bradley called, rooted to the spot.

He showed the sheriff the open door, drawer and window, then left him in the kitchen, moving through the rest of the house to look for anything that might be out of place.

Moments later Bradley Dobbins came charging back into the kitchen, calling out to the sheriff, his eyes wide and scared.

"Arlen, you gotta come see this," the vet insisted, heading back down the hall.

Bemis sighed and put his hands on his knees, pushing himself up to a standing position. He'd been crouched by the door, looking for telltale signs of forced entry. The out-of-shape lawman lumbered toward the bedroom, wondering why in the hell criminals didn't cause trouble during normal business hours. It was getting late, he was tired, and there was a smooth bourbon waiting at home.

Arlen made a face when Dobbins gestured to the magazine on the bed. A crude phallus had been drawn in lotion on the centerfold.

"Well, that makes me think that all of this trouble was caused by a teenager on a dare," Bemis shook his head.

"If it was, he's a dangerous teenager now," Dobbins growled.

"What's that supposed to mean?" the sheriff narrowed his eyes.

"Whoever it was...took my gun. I keep it in the drawer, and it's gone. They looked in my closet too. The light was on when I came in here, and I never leave the lights on."

"Well, that changes things," Arlen sighed, visions of paperwork dancing in his head. "See if you find anything else. I'm gonna have a deputy come in and take your statement. I've got deputies in cars and on foot combing the neighborhood, but you'll want to make sure that you lock up tight after we're done here."

Dobbins nodded.

"Do you think I should go check out my office building?" the vet asked.

"Nah, stuff like this usually isn't personal. You're a well-liked guy, I'm sure this was just a random thing. You probably won't have any more issues, but be alert for a while when you're coming and going," Arlen advised.

"I'm never going to get back to sleep tonight,"

Dobbins muttered, absent-mindedly shoving Oscar aside with his foot when the blissfully unaware animal moved in for some affection.

The cat hissed a warning, gave his owner a dirty look and sashayed from the room. Somewhere in the closet was a pair of sandals that needed to be peed on.

Susannah was positively giddy after her experiences at Bradley Dobbins' house. Tackling the meddling old man was something that she felt somewhat badly about, but the clues that she had left at the veterinarian's house would be driving both him and the police crazy, and the thought of all of those puzzled authority figures made her smile. Knowing that they were squirming with unsatisfied curiosity and righteous indignation gave her intense pleasure, and she toyed with the idea of merely tormenting the veterinarian for a while before killing him. His skin was nothing special, so that part could wait, but he'd pushed his luck too far for a permanent reprieve. She'd play for a while, but when she got bored, she'd kill him in a spectacularly appropriate fashion. What that would look like, she had no idea, as yet, but there was time to plot and plan, despite the bloodlust that rose up within her at the mere thought of the arrogant veterinarian.

Susannah had come home and stripped out of her "play clothes," putting them in the washing machine after hiding Bradley's gun behind the false back of a jelly cupboard in the basement. She'd shaken her hair free and gone upstairs to enjoy her bath, her mind racing with tantalizing possibilities for his death scene.

CHAPTER 18

Susannah was in a fantastic mood, until she arrived at work. She'd been fantasizing all morning about different ways to euthanize the arrogant veterinarian, and which souvenirs that she should claim afterwards, for her art collection. He had very large ears, which she might be able to make into a sort of leather flower to adorn the base of her skin tree. She was preoccupied with the details of how she could sew the skin into place to shape her flower, when she walked into Andre's spotless commercial kitchen and saw an unfamiliar face.

Andre was having a conversation with a young man who was dressed in the traditional black and white hounds-tooth pants, black jacket and white hat of an upper-level kitchen employee. The Head Chef beckoned to Susannah when she came in the door.

"Tanner, this is Susannah. She's my Assistant Chef, so you'll be doing whatever she instructs you to do. Susannah, this is one of our new prep guys, Tanner," Andre performed a quick introduction and the young man stuck out a limp hand, which Susannah shook... very briefly.

"Where's Rosa?" she frowned. Rosa was precise and fast, so even though she was a chatterbox, Susannah worked very well with her.

"She had some sort of family emergency, and the guy who works her opposite days quit, so we hired some additional guys to help pick up the slack."

Susannah stared at him, blinking. She hated new people. New people needed to be trained, and she hated training. She desperately hoped that this guy, and any others whom Andre had given a job, wouldn't want to engage in small talk. She despised small talk, particularly in the workplace. She'd only tolerated it from Rosa because the woman had extraordinary knife skills.

"Don't worry about training, I spent a couple of hours

last night, and the entire morning bringing him up to speed and he's a pretty quick study, so we should get through the lunch rush just fine, and then we'll have one of the seasoned guys work with him tonight so he can get a feel for dinner prep," Andre assured Susannah, noting the glazed look in her eyes. "We got fourteen cases of rabbits in that need to be prepared. If you want to get started, I'll have Tanner work the vegetables."

"Okay," she nodded, brightening a bit at the thought of being able to precisely dismember the rabbits, her cleaver making cuts so perfect that each piece would look just like the others.

Susannah had sliced and diced her way through three of the pink creatures before Tanner came back from the massive commercial fridge with a large bin filled with veggies, and set himself up at an adjacent work station. She was glad that he didn't seem to be much of a talker, but was a bit unnerved by the way that he watched her. He peeled and chopped with a skill that nearly matched hers, all the while sneaking glances at her peripherally.

"You're really good at that," Tanner said quietly, not looking at her.

She studied him for a moment, trying not to stare at the artfully arranged bun which sat atop his head beneath the required hair net. He seemed rather like a hipster version of Tim.

"I've had lots of practice," she shrugged.

"Me too," he said mildly. "Do you want some help with that? I'm actually better with flesh than with plants."

Susannah didn't look up from her work, but wondered at the slight thrill that shot through her when he said that.

"No, I'm good. Thanks though."

"No problem."

The two of them worked in silence, each intent upon their task, and she had to admit that she was impressed, and somehow intrigued by the new employee. So much so that, despite her disdain for small talk, she initiated a conversation.

"So, you must have a good amount of experience in the kitchen," Susannah commented, for once wanting to know more about a fellow human being.

"Nope, not really."

She stared at him, surprised that someone seemed less inclined to talk than she.

"What did you do before this?"

"I just moved here from out of state. I was in…healthcare."

"Healthcare?"

"Yes ma'am."

"Don't call me ma'am, it makes me feel responsible," a corner of Susannah's mouth quirked up in a slight smile.

The truth was that when she heard the term "ma'am," it made her think of her mother, and that never turned out well.

"Sorry," Tanner glanced up from his work only briefly.

"It's okay. So what brought you to Pellman?" she persisted, odd behavior for her.

The young man shrugged.

"Dunno. Never been here before, seemed like it might be interesting."

"Interesting? Never heard Pellman described that way before. Well, I hope everything works out for you. It looks like you're going to do just fine here, if you continue to work like that," she pointed at his growing pile of prep work with her cleaver.

"Thanks."

Tanner and Susannah breezed through the lunch rush like they'd worked together their entire lives. Little was said, but much was accomplished, and when Andre asked her how the new kid was working out, she replied with more enthusiasm than the Head Chef had ever seen from her. At the end of their shift, she tossed her apron into the hamper and regarded him with a measure of respect.

"Good job in there today."

"Thanks, you too," Tanner sat on a chair in the break-room, tying his shoe, but stood and followed Susannah out the door when she left.

She started walking home and realized that he was right behind her. Stopping, she turned.

"You live around here?" she asked, not unnerved in the slightest.

"Couple miles from here."

"Me too," she nodded. "Whereabouts?"

"Slidell Street, in the apartments across from the gas station."

The area was right between where Pellman turned from respectable to seedy, home to those who were still willing to struggle enough to keep from going under.

"That's a few blocks from my house," Susannah commented, glad that she lived on the more comfortable side of town. "You'll go right past my place to get there. I live next door to the mortuary."

"That must be cool," Tanner replied, falling in step beside her, hands shoved in his pockets.

She shot a quick glance at him to see if he was mocking her, but he didn't seem to be.

"Sometimes," she murmured.

A squirrel skittered across their path, and the young man's eyes followed it, making Susannah's heart speed up a bit. She knew that look…she'd seen it before, and she stared at the quiet young man as they walked, trying to figure him out. He stopped walking and stared at her without expression.

"What?" he asked, sounding more curious than defensive.

"Nothing," she shook her head and kept walking. He fell back into step. "You like animals?" she asked casually.

A non-committal shrug was the only response.

"Got any pets?" she tried again.

"No."

"Le Chateau isn't your only job, is it, Tanner?"

"Nope."

"Where else do you work?" the introverted chef was quite the inquisitor at the moment, stepping out of her self-imposed shell to find out more about this young man who inexplicably fascinated her.

"Dr. Dobbins' office."

A slow smile slid across Susannah's face, as she put two and two together.

"You like it there?"

Another shrug. "It's money."

"How do you feel about your boss?"

Another sidelong glance from the young man.

"He's okay, I guess. He's only there for the money too."

"What do you mean?"

"He gives really sick animals these bogus "supplements," when they really should just be put out of their misery. The stuff is really expensive, and if you read the ingredient list, it's just like a bunch of chopped up weeds or something."

"What kind of person would do such a thing?" Susannah wondered, watching Tanner closely.

"I don't judge."

"I don't either, but don't you wish you could…do something? To help the poor animals, I mean."

Tanner flashed her a brief look, a hunger in his eyes

that was more than familiar, but he masked the look as quickly as he could.

"I'm not the doctor. Nothing I can do. I just clean cages and stock shelves and stuff."

"Still must be hard to see," she mused, letting it go.

He didn't respond, and they walked the remaining few blocks in companionable silence.

"Well, this is me," she inclined her head toward the cozy cottage that she shared with an undertaker.

"Cool," Tanner nodded. "See ya," he said, and ambled toward the scary side of town.

CHAPTER 19

"So where was the mortuary freak when my house was violated?" Bradley Dobbins demanded, sitting across from Sheriff Arlen Bemis in a local café.

"He has an air-tight alibi for that night. He was hosting a wake at the mortuary, and has scores of witnesses who can testify that they never saw him leave. His story checks out," Arlen shrugged, taking a swig of thick black coffee.

"Then he put somebody up to it," the vet insisted.

"You're soundin a mite paranoid there, Dobbins."

"Well, who else could it be?"

"A kid looking for cash, most likely," Bemis crossed

his arms over his chest and gazed at his breakfast companion steadily.

"I wonder if it's the new kid that got hired at my office. There's something squirrely about him."

"Ya know, it ain't healthy to be suspicious of every person who crosses your path. Random is usually just that...random. Just cuz your house got broken into don't mean that somebody's out to get you, Brad. Relax. Conscience gettin' ya?" the sheriff smirked.

"My conscience is just fine, thank you very much," the vet snipped.

The sheriff waved a hand.

"I don't get you animal people. Why you'd want to have a critter living inside with you is beyond me, but I know there's a market for that sort of thing. Just do your wildlife witch doctor voodoo and let me worry about crime. You should be just fine," Arlen exercised extreme self-control and didn't roll his eyes.

"I still think there's something strange going on with the mortician and his odd wife," Bradley mused.

"Yeah, and your house is probably haunted too," the

sheriff mocked him, refusing to even listen to that type of conversation.

He drank the last grit-filled dregs of his badly burnt coffee and set the cup down on the table, rising to go.

"So you're not going to investigate any further? Do I really have to take matters into my own hands?" the vet asked, eyebrow raised in challenge.

Arlen Bemis put both fists on the table and bent over, speaking in a low voice.

"You'd better not be taking anything into your own hands, hear me? The investigation is still open, and when we get any leads, I'll let you know. In the meantime, go peddle your doggie vitamins and leave the mortician alone. He may be a strange character, but he ain't done nothin' to ya. Am I being fairly clear here, Brad?"

"Yeah, yeah, I got it," the vet dismissed him with a grimace. "Doesn't mean that I agree though."

"Ain't no need for agreement," Arlen smirked. "Just let me alone and I'll get it figured out."

"I know you will, Bemis. I'm sorry," Brad ran a frustrated hand through his hair. "I just get so mad at the thought of someone messing with me."

"Don't sweat the small stuff. I got this," the sheriff declared with supreme confidence, digging in his olive green pants pocket for his keys.

"I hope so, Arlen. I really do."

The vet watched his friend and ally leave, and tossed his sticky fork onto the remainder of his pancakes, suddenly not hungry. He planned to have dinner at Le Chateau again, in order to facilitate another encounter with Susannah Eckels, the mortician's wife. He didn't know what it was about this couple that fascinated him so, but they both gave him the creeps and he had to find out why.

"You want a more interesting prep job?" Susannah asked Tanner as he tied the strings of his apron behind him.

"Whatcha got in mind?" the young man asked, mildly interested.

"We got a shipment of lambs in today. We're going to make rack of lamb as a dinner feature, but we also need to cut chops off of them, and make whatever's left into a spiced minced meat for a Moroccan dish that I'll be making next week. You think you're skilled enough to tackle whole lambs? I figured with your knowledge of animal anatomy and meats, you'd probably know exactly what to do."

Tanner's eyes lit up for a brief moment, before his perpetual mask came slamming back into place.

"Uh, yeah, I could do it," he nodded, making a feeble attempt at nonchalance.

Susannah led him to the cold storage, noting that when he worked the admission bar to the unit, his hands were shaking slightly.

"Too much caffeine?"

"Yeah, I guess," the young man replied with a nervous chuckle.

He lifted the first carcass gently down from the hook upon which it had been hung when the butcher delivered it, and carried it out into the kitchen, setting it down on the prep surface gently, almost reverently. Susannah walked him through the cuts that he needed to make, then left him to his slicing and dicing, silver blades flashing.

"You're a natural," she observed, heading back to her station.

"It just comes easily to me, I guess," Tanner murmured, absorbed in his task. He was busy for the rest of his shift, and when she checked his work, she wasn't surprised to find it flawless, the cuts perfect.

Susannah and Tanner headed home at the same time, falling into step naturally.

"You did a good job today," she complimented him.

"Thanks."

"How's your other job going?"

The young man was silent for a moment, but it seemed clear that something was on his mind.

"There's this dog…" he began, then shook his head. "I don't even know why I care, but he's this big guy.

He used to be a tough dude, you can just tell…and now his owner has to put a towel across his belly and lift up the back of him so that he can walk and go to the bathroom," Tanner muttered, his jaw clenching and unclenching, as though he were wrestling with the subject.

"That's too bad," Susannah commented. "How old is he?"

"Almost fifteen."

"Does that mean that he's going to…?" she let the question hang between them.

"Die? Yeah, I suppose, but, even though his hips gave out, his body, and his…like…spirit are still strong, ya know?" he shook his head in disgust.

"Sounds like he must be miserable."

"You can see it in his eyes, ya know?"

"Is he getting the supplements?"

"Of course. They just don't do anything."

"I might be able to help."

"Huh?"

Susannah told Tanner about what Tim had done, first for Shelby's cat, and then for Rosa's dog, and the youth took it all in, nodding occasionally, but mostly looking very solemn.

"Does it hurt?"

"No, he just makes them go to sleep and they don't wake up. Do you have any way to talk to the owners?"

Tanner nodded.

"When they get dropped off for treatments, I take them back, and when they get picked up, I put them in the owners' cars."

"So, maybe you could tell some of them about Tim, and…what he does," Susannah suggested.

"Maybe," he fell silent. Just as they arrived in front of the mortuary, he stopped on the sidewalk, and looked at his boss carefully. "Why do you care?" he asked without accusation.

Susannah shrugged. "I had to take care of the animals that my family had when we had this small farm. I never allowed an animal to suffer on my watch. If they needed to die to provide food for us, I helped them die…and then we ate them. It was a win-win."

Tanner's eyes narrowed slightly, and he merely nodded.

"Okay. See you tomorrow," he said, continuing on his way.

CHAPTER 20

Bradley Dobbins was going to be late for work, which normally didn't upset him, but the reason that he was going to be late was particularly irritating.

"Oscar? Oscar, where are you?" he tried to coo, angry that his feline companion had chosen this rather inconvenient time to hide from him.

"Oscar?" he called out again and again as he looked under beds, behind furniture and in every nook, cranny and crevice in his sizeable house. Oscar wasn't an outdoor cat, so he had to be in the house somewhere.

When the veterinarian stepped into his mudroom, a chill ran down his spine, and he grimaced. The door to the garage was ajar. He locked it every night before bedtime. Stepping out into the grey realm of oil, gas and cut grass, he saw immediately that the side door to the garage was wide open, letting in sunlight and fresh air, and undoubtedly letting out poor fat little Oscar.

Dobbins jogged out into the side yard from the garage, calling Oscar's name, then listening for a familiar meow. Nothing. He looked under bushes, in window wells, and in trees, but there was no sign of Oscar. Gritting his teeth and letting out an exasperated sigh, he called Sheriff Arlen Bemis to report yet another break in.

Tanner was skillfully removing the skin and bones from a heaping pile of catfish when Susannah arrived at Le Chateau.

"Wow, you're making quick work of that," she commented, with an approving nod.

"Lots of practice," the young man replied, focused on his task.

"Oh? You fish?"

Tanner's flashing knife stilled for a moment, and he cocked his head, looking at her, puzzled.

"No."

"Can I ask you a question?" the normally reticent Susannah couldn't contain her fascination with the new prep cook.

"I guess," he shrugged, grabbing another fish.

She stepped a bit closer and looked around before speaking quietly.

"What happens when things don't go well at Dr. Dobbins' office and an animal can't be saved? What happens when it...expires?"

Tanner's eyes darted back and forth briefly, before he regained focus, not looking at his boss.

"That depends."

"On?"

"The owner's wishes, usually. Some people want to take them home and bury them, so we check their address to make sure that they live in a part of town where that's allowed. If they can't bury them, but want the ashes, we can freeze the body and send it off to a company who cremates it and sends it back in a pretty box or jar."

Susannah stepped closer, so close that she could almost hear the inhale and exhale of the nervous young man in front of her.

"What happens when the owners don't want to have anything to do with the remains?"

Tanners knife stilled for a moment, but then he seemed to attack the flesh in front of him with more determination.

"We take them out to the ovens at the landfill and they cremate them. They have a separate bio section out there, kind of like a pet cemetery, but it's all one big grave," he explained.

"And do you, personally, ever deliver the bodies to the landfill?" she asked quietly, her voice a caress.

"Sometimes."

"And do you ever…make stops along the way?" half of her mouth quirked up into a smile.

"I don't know what…" Tanner's knife faltered, and he swallowed convulsively.

"Shhh…" she put a hand on his arm. "It's okay…I get it," she whispered. "I have hobbies too."

The young man turned to his boss then, eyes wide, knife glinting in the glare of commercial lighting, and Susannah felt a rush of excitement.

"I think we have a lot in common, you and I," a slow grin spread across her face.

The hunger within her was fierce. No one had tried to impose their will on Susannah in a very long time, but the need to claim a life rose up within her like hot lava on the verge of spewing out death and destruction. The blood in her veins hummed with need, and she couldn't help but wonder if it might not be because she'd found a sort of kindred spirit in Tanner. She didn't know what dark secrets the young man held, but she sensed something within him that was similar to her own dark needs. The way he held his knife, his quiet disinterest in humanity, his shy awkward manner…they all spoke to her. Something about him connected with something about her, in ways that she didn't quite understand…yet.

"Susannah!" Andre bellowed, shattering her reverie.

"What?"

"Table 17. Get out there, let him thank you for your outstanding culinary skills, then get back here and work on the crème brulee," the Head Chef ordered, jerking his head toward the dining room as he added a dash of wine to a sautéed dish, making it flame briefly.

"Do I have..." she began, making a face.

"Just hurry up, it won't kill you. Smile, shake his hand, say thank you, and get it over with. Go," Andre waved a hand at her.

Sighing, she snapped off her gloves, wiped her hands on a kitchen towel and headed for the dining room. Her expression darkened briefly when she saw the occupant of Table 17, Dr. Bradley Dobbins. Again.

"Hello," she hoped her half smile looked more convincing than it felt.

"Good evening. I just wanted to tell you how much I enjoyed my entrée," he gestured at his nearly full plate.

"All two bites of it?" she didn't even attempt to hold back the snarky comment that rose to her lips.

"I'm a light eater," he shrugged, oozing confidence. "I met your husband. Interesting fellow," he gazed at her darkly, knowingly.

"Great. Well, I'm glad you enjoyed your dinner. I need to get back to the…" she began, but Dobbins sat forward and cut her off.

"It's only a matter of time before I take him down," he whispered, with a pleasant smile. "He thinks he's good at playing games, but he doesn't realize that I WILL win this one."

Susannah's face went slack, and it took considerable restraint for her to not grab the arrogant bastard's steak knife from the table and plunge it into the nearest artery. Her need raged through her, and her vision briefly swam with a red miasma as she fantasized about a slow, painful death for the veterinarian. She swayed a bit, and he grinned, taking her reaction as a sign of weakness. If he'd really known what emotions were flooding through her at the moment, he'd have been smart to run for the hills.

"Your move," she whispered, and stared at him with a

look so evil that he was taken aback for a moment, his supreme confidence faltering.

She left him at a loss for words, maintaining eye contact while she slowly turned away and headed for the kitchen.

CHAPTER 21

Timothy Eckels had settled into his role as town mortician remarkably easily. As the owner of the only funeral home in town, he had a steady stream of business, and had received some very positive endorsements from grateful townsfolk. Most of the deaths that he dealt with were from various accidents or old age, and life was running along rather smoothly for the mild-mannered mortician. He'd just finished putting the final touches on a seventy-nine year old retired school teacher, whose funeral promised to be a town-wide event, when he heard the front door chime sound. Sighing, he snapped off his gloves and went to see who had entered his cool, quiet realm.

"You need to help my Elmo," a pinch-faced woman in

a pink suit declared, when Tim came into view at the top of the basement stairs, giving the mortician a look that brooked no nonsense.

"Excuse me?" Tim blinked at the high-energy society matron. He hadn't received any calls for a body pickup, he would've remembered a deceased person named Elmo.

"The young man from the vet clinic told me that you could...help me with...something," the woman looked uncomfortable, but her demanding gaze never wavered.

"Young man? I'm afraid I don't understand," the mortician frowned, baffled.

The woman crossed her arms and tapped her foot. "I need help with Elmo, my geriatric Irish Setter," she explained, raising an eyebrow in a manner that seemed like a challenge.

"Shouldn't you see the vet about that?"

"I have seen the vet about that," she mocked him tersely. "And he won't do what needs to be done. I understand that you can take care of things that the vet won't."

Light dawned on the mortician finally, and he held up his hands, shaking his head.

"Oh, I think you have the wrong person. I don't have anything to do with animals. I don't even own a pet," Tim backed away.

The woman's face darkened like an impending storm.

"Don't toy with me, Mr. Eckels. I know precisely what you do, and I'd hate to have to go to the sheriff and talk with him about that," she said lightly, examining her nails with a haughty air that Tim found offensive to the extreme. "You help me with my… issue, and I'll keep quiet. My husband plays golf with the District Attorney, you know," she smiled tightly.

"Surely you can afford to go to a professional who can give you what you want," Timothy Eckels stared at her, aghast.

"Of course I can, but the nearest "professional" is at least a two hour drive away, and I don't have that kind of time to waste. Now are you going to take care of Elmo, or do I have to visit the Sheriff's office?" she glanced at her watch.

Tim's eyes darted back and forth as he wracked his

brain, trying to think of an alternative to offer this horrendous woman, but he came up with nothing.

"Fine," the woman snipped, whirling toward the exit. "I guess I'll just go see..."

"Wait!" Tim interrupted, clearly displeased. "Drive around to the cargo bay in the back. I'll take him down on the elevator."

"Wise choice," was the obnoxious reply.

Tim locked the front and side doors, making absolutely certain that no one could enter the mortuary while he took the ailing animal to the basement, then headed for the loading dock, hoping that the Setter wasn't large. He wasn't capable of carrying a great deal of dead weight, and didn't want to drop the poor dying creature. He opened up the cargo bay door at the back of the Victorian just as the rude woman opened the back door of her fine German automobile.

"Get out here," she reached in, jerking on a red nylon leash.

The most beautiful, glossy Irish Setter that Tim had ever seen, bounded from the car, looking this way and that, and shying away from the woman who held the leash. Spotting Tim, Elmo lunged, ripping the leash out of his owner's hand, and bounding over to the startled mortician, who actually cracked a smile when the exuberant red dog planted his paws on Tim's shoulders and started licking his face.

"He doesn't seem sick," Tim observed, gently pushing the affectionate dog down, and grabbing the leash.

"He has seizures," was the reply. Her look dared the mortician to challenge her claim.

"How old is he? Maybe with medication…"

"I told you, medication doesn't help. He's suffering horribly," she insisted, glancing down at the floppy-eared animal who was wagging his graceful plume of a tail against Tim's leg.

Tim stared at the woman, thinking that this must be what pure evil looked like.

"What's to become of the remains?" he swallowed, a plan forming in the back of his mind.

"I'll have the young man from the vet clinic come by

to pick him up when you're done. How long will this take?"

"Not long, but…won't it be rather…risky for you to involve someone else?"

"Of course not. I told you, he referred me here. He obviously isn't going to tell anyone," the woman waved dismissively.

Glancing down at the perfectly healthy-looking dog again, she bent forward to pat the animal on the head, and Elmo cringed away, burrowing his face in the leg of Tim's chinos.

"Good riddance," she muttered, backing away without having touched him.

Tim stood silently, holding Elmo's leash, as she got back into her car and drove away, without so much as a backward glance. The dog looked up at the mortician, with a wide doggy grin.

"What are we going to do with you, I wonder?" Tim mused, smiling faintly when Elmo nuzzled his hand.

Until he could think of a viable solution, Tim led the dog into the elevator and took him down to the basement. The thought of euthanizing a joyful, perfectly healthy dog like Elmo brought bile to the back of his throat, and he couldn't bring himself to even think about mixing up his special sleep cocktail. He grabbed a clean fluid collection bin from a supply cabinet and filled it with water for the animal, placing it on the floor next to a blanket, so that the dog could lie down while he figured out what to do with him.

A pair of big, brown canine eyes followed Tim to and fro as he resumed working on the school teacher, hoping that the tasks would clear his head enough to inspire him with a solution for the Elmo dilemma. Focused on the final stages of his preparation, he heard the doorbell buzzing out front, and remembered that he'd locked all entrances to the mortuary before taking Elmo to the basement.

"Stay," he whispered to the lovely dog, who obediently laid his head on his paws, seemingly content to stay on his blanket.

A quiet young man with his hair in a messy ponytail stood on the porch in front of the mortuary.

"Yes?" Tim frowned, irritated at the disruption of his work, yet again.

"I'm Tanner," was the mild reply from the youth who

stood with his hands jammed firmly into the pockets of his jeans.

"And?" Tim sighed, in no mood for guessing games.

"I'm here to pick up Elmo," Tanner leaned in and whispered.

"Oh." Tim studied him carefully. "Have you ever met Elmo?"

"Yeah, he gets boarded with us when his owners go on vacation or travel for business."

"So, you're aware that there's nothing wrong with Elmo, right?"

Tanner nodded, his eyes sad.

"Do you have pets?"

"No. I just moved here."

"Do you like animals?"

"Absolutely," the young man's face was without guile.

"Do you think it would be possible for you to take Elmo and give him a good home? If you can't, I understand, but I'm not...I just...I'll find him another home."

"You'd do that?"

"I don't see an alternative."

"I'll take him," Tanner said quietly. "Where is he?"

"This way," Tim opened the door wider, letting the young man in, then took him to the basement.

When Tanner came into the work area, he stopped in his tracks, his eyes fixed on the school teacher that Tim had been working on.

"Is that real?" he asked, wide-eyed, but not the least bit squeamish.

"Quite so. Elmo is over here."

At the sound of his name, the dog stood, wagging his tail and looking happily from Tim to Tanner and back again. Tanner sank down to his knees, and held out a hand to the dog, who trotted over, slathering the young man in sloppy kisses.

"He knows you," Tim remarked, puzzled that, rather than petting the animal, Tanner seemed to be inspecting him rather clinically. He watched him examine the dog's eyes, ears, tail, and musculature, figuring that it was something he did at the vet clinic.

"Yeah, he does." Tanner stood, taking Elmo's leash.

"He seems like a nice dog," the mortician offered, not knowing what to say. "Do you need a ride home?"

"Nah, we're good," the thin young man replied, once again staring at the cadaver in the room with them. "What are you going to do with that?" he asked.

"Let a few hundred people pay their last respects, then bury him," Tim shrugged.

Tanner looked at the mortician curiously and nodded.

"Gotta go," the young man said, taking one last look at the corpse.

"Bye Elmo," Tim said soberly, patting the dog on the head.

Susannah came home from work and went directly to the basement of their cozy cottage. Tim was in bed long before she was done working on whatever current art project she had, and she snuggled up to him in the wee hours of the night, content for the moment. The busy Assistant Chef was still asleep the next morning when her husband got up to start his day.

Tim sat down at the kitchen table with his bowl of oatmeal, being careful not to make too much noise, so that his wife could sleep. When he finished his breakfast, and had brushed his teeth, he noticed that Susannah's sweater was draped over the back of a dining room chair. Thinking that she might want it later for her walk to work he picked it up and hung it in the closet. He was about to turn away, when a thin line on one sleeve caught his eye. Gingerly picking up the sleeve, he brought it closer, so that he could see it, and his heart beat faster when he realized what he was looking at.

There, on his wife's sweater, was a medium-length mahogany-colored hair, that looked coincidentally like it had come from the Irish Setter he'd spent time with yesterday. This was the second time this month that there had been a hair on Susannah that didn't belong to her, and he couldn't help but wonder how the hairs were getting on her clothing. He told himself that it had to be accidental. Perhaps she had brushed by someone at the grocery store, or maybe someone at work had borrowed her apron, getting a hair on it, which then transferred to her clothing, but a deep, dark feeling wriggled and squiggled in the pit of his stomach, and he dropped the sleeve, leaving the closet.

CHAPTER 22

Susannah walked home alone today, it was Tanner's day off, and she figured that the young man was busy with an art project of his own. Seeing Elmo, when the young man had come by the restaurant to collect his paycheck, had inspired her to be on the lookout for a redhead to add to her materials. The freckled skin would make interesting leaves, and the hair would add a brilliant touch of color. Her eyes were still on the prize, Dr. Bradley Dobbins, but he was her long game, she needed a quick fix and decided that she might as well go with a skin type that she hadn't encountered before.

There was a lovely ginger cheerleader named Abigail Sorenson at the high school, who had been in the newspaper last week because she had raised money for a local charity, but Susannah knew better than to assume that she was a good person just because her face was splashed all over the news. She was a cheerleader, which meant, by definition, that she looked down upon others who were not of her social class, and that her life had been a series of easy opportunities and moments of good fortune thrown at her feet, simply because she was pretty and popular. She probably threw tantrums, demanded to get her way, and hurt whomever she needed to in order to stay on top, Susannah knew the type all too well.

She'd posed as a mother and called the school that morning to see what time cheerleading practice ended. Just before the group called it quits for the day, Susannah had stationed herself along the route that she knew Abigail would take on the way home, waiting. She'd scoped out the place where she'd take the young lady to turn her into art materials, and figured out a plan to lure her there. When she saw the young lady strolling down the sidewalk, alone, she collapsed, crying out in pain. Abigail saw her go down and ran over.

"Oh my gosh, are you okay?" the cheerleader asked, green eyes wide. "Should I call an ambulance or something?" She pulled out her cell phone and Susannah knew that she had to strike quickly.

"No, please...don't call an ambulance," she writhed on the sidewalk, holding her knee as though injured. "I can't afford to go to the hospital, I don't have insurance."

"Do you need a ride? I could ask my dad..."

"No, that's really sweet of you," Susannah spoke quickly, wanting to get off of the street before anyone could see them interacting. "I live right on the other side of the woods over there," she pointed. "Do you think you could maybe help me get to my house? I can walk with a little support," she grimaced.

"Oh yeah, of course," Abigail nodded, swinging her backpack down from her shoulder and putting her cell phone and water bottle inside.

She slid both arms back through the straps, and bent down to offer a hand. Susannah pretended to let the teenager help her up, then began hobbling toward the woods, which she had combed earlier, looking for the most private, out-of-the-way spot to do what needed to be done.

"Does it hurt much?" Abigail worried, a concerned frown on her smooth, freckled face.

"It seems to get better as I move," Susannah grunted, leaning on the girl a bit, knowing that having to support her weight would wear Abigail out, making her weaker.

"Oh, that's great! I hope you're going to be okay."

"I'll need to rest a bit when I get home, but I'll be fine," she had to repress a smile that flickered around the corners of her mouth. "At the hollow tree over there, cut to the right, it's the shortest way."

"Really? I didn't know there were any houses out this way," Abigail remarked, trying to make conversation to take Susannah's mind off of the pain.

"It's new construction," she huffed, wincing, playing her part.

"How nice," the cheerleader smiled, her moist skin pink from exertion.

Susannah looked at the glowing skin and wished there was some way that she could make it stay that color. The pink blush on the white skin, with chocolatey freckles reminded her of Neopolitan ice cream. She loved Neopolitan ice cream.

"Go to the left by those big rocks over there," she instructed, knowing that there was a nice little enclosed space on the other side of the rocks, made by the intersection of two rock formations and shielded by a thick patch of undergrowth.

"Wow, this looks like a fairyland," Abigail smiled when they went around the rocks.

"Where all your dreams come true," Susannah cooed, moving lightning-fast from beneath Abigail's arm and putting a choke hold on her before the clueless teenager could utter a sound.

She couldn't see her face, but she knew that her bulging eyes would be open wide with terror, her nostrils would be flaring as the realization that she'd soon be taking her last breath hit, and her mouth would be agape with a soundless scream.

The cheerleader was fit, and strong, but she only weighed a little over a hundred pounds, and her wiry frame was no match for the strapping woman who muscled her past the undergrowth, into the roughly six-by-six clearing in between the rocks, where she'd have privacy. Susannah patiently held on, the guttural grunts of Abigail trying desperately to catch her breath finally subsiding. When the girl went limp, her killer lowered her to the ground, and, while still unconscious, her lungs sucked in air automatically. Susannah pulled her gloves out of her jeans pocket and slid them on, then placed several strips of duct tape over the teenager's nose and mouth, so that she'd die of asphyxiation.

Abigail struggled briefly, but succumbed with a dramatic relaxing of her muscles eventually. Susannah surveyed the beautiful specimen in front of her with a clinical eye. She wanted a different look and feel for her leaves, so she examined the girl's body carefully, choosing just the right spots for excision. She noticed that the girl's eyelids had finer, paler freckles, and realized that if she took the entire upper eyelid, she'd have beautiful ginger brow hairs on one side of her leaf, and sweetly curled eyelashes on the other. For a sense of symmetry, she took the other eyelid too, placing both pieces of flesh in a plastic baggie. Brilliant orbs of green stared up at the early Fall sky, and Susannah found herself wishing that she could somehow incorporate that color into one of her pieces, but she didn't waste much time thinking about it, there was other harvesting to be done.

She had just removed a patch of scalp with a long lock of glorious red hair attached, when she heard a crashing in the bushes and the sound of laughter close by. Too close by. Susannah held her breath, frozen in place. There were two young boys, judging by the sound of their laughter, and they were moving fast enough that they had to be on bikes. She'd picked this spot because it was difficult to get to, and was furious that her activity had been interrupted. She thought seriously about jumping out into the open and killing them both, but if she was busy with one and the other happened to get away, that could spell disaster, so she waited, crouched, as they moved rapidly closer.

Susannah heard their sweet young voices, and could smell the tang of their sweat, as they pedaled their bikes as fast as they dared through the undeveloped terrain. Only when she heard them whiz by without a second glance, did she release the breath that she hadn't known she'd been holding. Some of the joy of her task had ebbed, though adrenalin rocketed through her body, but she went back to it, hurrying this time.

The skin on Abigail's foot was so thin that it appeared to be transparent, and Susannah just had to have some of it. After securing her materials, she put the teenager's shoe back on and surveyed her baggies of materials. Satisfied that she had enough from the lovely teenager, she dragged what was left of Abigail Sorenson into a crevice under one of the rocks, rolled her over so that she lay on her face, because the staring eyes freaked her out a little bit, and peeled off her gloves, putting them in a plastic grocery sack to dispose of later.

The sun was sinking fast, and the temperature had dropped, causing Susannah to shiver a bit, despite her activity. She wanted to get out of the woods quickly, her feet hurt from wearing shoes that she'd stolen from a homeless man behind a grocery store, and she wanted a nice hot bath before Tim came home.

With this particular victim, she was glad that she didn't have to worry about blood spatter, because the work that she had done was post-mortem. She typically liked to see the pulsing and spurting of blood from a live victim, and take her samples as their life force ebbed from their body, but today had been about satiating her appetite in the most efficient way possible. It was going to be torture for her to wait for these leaves to dry. She'd place them in a position of importance upon her tree, for, while it hadn't been a spectacular kill, it had been satisfying enough, and the materials were glorious. Feeling smug and titillated over a job well-done, she headed home to shower. She'd make Timothy a nice meal, then have her way with him. On the floor. Maybe even with candles.

CHAPTER 23

Timothy Eckels looked up from his desk, disheartened to see Sheriff Arlen Bemis staring down at him grimly. Tim had been so absorbed in his perusal of a forensics article online, that he hadn't heard him come in.

"Hello Sheriff," he greeted him mildly.

"You've got a lot of explaining to do, mister," the sheriff chomped on his toothpick like his life depended on it.

Tim sighed, not caring that the lawman saw his obvious annoyance.

"What now?"

The sheriff roughly pulled back one of the club chairs

in front of Tim's desk and sat down hard, leaning toward the mortician over the desk.

"If you think this is a game, you're sadly mistaken," he growled.

"I have no idea what you're talking about," Tim folded his hands on the desk and stared.

"Where were you last night?"

"Depends."

"On what?" Arlen's eyes narrowed.

"On when. I was at certain places at certain times."

"Well, why don't you start from about five o'clock and tell me everywhere that you were from that point on, and you better watch that attitude," the sheriff threatened.

"I don't have attitudes," Tim commented dryly. "At five o'clock, I was setting up for the wake of Harper McClellan, he's the...."

"I know who Harper is, get to the rest of it," Bemis ordered.

"Guests started showing up around six-thirty, and I

was hosting the viewing until after ten o'clock. It was supposed to end at nine-thirty, but then his sister fainted and I…"

"Yeah, yeah, I get it. Then where did you go?"

"Home."

"I'll need a list of guests who were at the funeral," Arlen muttered.

"I can get you the guest book."

"Well, don't just sit there, go get it," the sheriff ordered, clearly upset about something.

Tim brought the book back and handed it to the sheriff.

"I'll get it back to ya, I'm taking it into evidence."

"Evidence? Evidence for what?"

"There was a young woman who died under suspicious circumstances last night, and we're just chasing down any leads that we might find helpful," Arlen hedged.

"You think someone at the funeral might have something to do with the crime?"

"Anything's possible," the sheriff stared hard at the mortician. "Tell me somethin'…do you take pictures of people before you work on 'em?"

"Yes, I take before and after photos," Tim nodded.

"You remember that car wreck victim last week, Lonnie Goins?"

"Yes, that was a challenge."

"Dig up them pictures for me. I wanna see 'em."

"Okay, but why?" the mortician asked reasonably, going to a file cabinet.

"Cuz I said so, freak-show," the sheriff raised an eyebrow.

Tim paused for a moment, giving Arlen a long look, but then turned to the file cabinet, opened a drawer, and extracted Lonnie's file. He pulled the before and after photos out and handed them to the sheriff.

"Nope, gimme the whole thing," Bemis held out his hand for the file.

"This information is confidential," Tim hesitated.

"Do you really want me to open up an investigation

of this place to gain access? That could shut you down for weeks, Eckels."

Tim was growing really tired of being threatened by this insufferable man, so, in the interest of getting rid of the sheriff, he handed over the file.

"What all ya got in here?"

"Notes about what I had to do, a materials list, invoices for products ordered, special requests from the family, that sort of thing."

Bemis laid the photos out with "befores" on the left, and "afters" on the right.

"How'd you get that gash to close up?" the sheriff asked, pointing to a raggedy laceration on the side of the corpse's face.

"I had to trim away the uneven pieces of skin, fat and muscle tissue, then sew the two halves together, and use a putty mixture to cover the seam," Tim explained, warming to the subject.

"That what this picture is, before you put the putty on?"

"Exactly. You can see why I can't leave it that way."

"Still pretty precise work though," the sheriff remarked. "Whatcha use to do the cuttin'?"

"It…uh…depends. For the fatty tissue and muscle, I used a short-bladed set of shears, and for the upper-most layers of skin, I use a scalpel and tweezers, usually."

"And this stuff don't turn your stomach?"

"Uh, no sheriff, it's my job."

"It sure is, isn't it? Business been good?"

"Very steady, yes."

"Not tempted to go out and make more victims are ya?"

The questions sounded like a joke, but the sheriff's face was entirely serious, leaving Tim confused.

"I don't find that funny," the mortician stated flatly.

"That's cuz it ain't funny. I'm gonna be watchin' you, Eckels. You can be sure of that," Arlen shoved the chair backward and stood up.

"Thank you?" Tim replied.

"Don't get smart," the sheriff warned.

"I wasn't. If people are out there dying under suspicious circumstances, I'm glad that you're going to be keeping an eye on me," the morticians gaze didn't waver for a second. "When can I come get the body?"

"After the coroner is done with it. Don't call us, we'll call you."

"Have a nice day," Tim blinked and pushed his thick glasses up his nose, going back to reading his article.

Arlen Bemis headed for the door, then turned back around, seeming to remember something.

"What size shoe do you wear?" he asked.

Tim stared at him blankly.

"Ten and a half, why?"

The sheriff shook his head.

"It figures, that'd be too easy," he muttered, and left the office.

"How was your day?" Tim asked his wife during dinner.

Susannah had brought home leftovers from work, and they were dining on a spectacular dish made with duck and garlic and something green that tasted delicious.

"Not bad, the usual. You?" she tossed the conversational ball back into his court, more interested in her food than in her husband.

"The sheriff came by to talk to me today. He took my guest book."

Susannah studied her plate like she was preparing for a test.

"Really? Why?" she took in a huge mouthful of duck.

"Apparently someone died under suspicious circumstances yesterday."

"How awful. Do they think it had something to do with the dead guy at the funeral?"

Tim was silent for a moment.

"I never thought of that, actually. I don't know why they would, the deceased passed due to natural causes. I didn't see anything suspicious about him at all."

"Do you generally look for suspicious things?" she finally looked up from her plate, fixing her gaze intently upon her husband.

"Every time," he nodded.

"Why?" Susannah put her fork down and took a sip of iced tea.

"Because I tend to catch things that coroners and medical examiners usually miss. I've helped solve a few cases. The body always tells the story if you look hard enough."

"Doesn't it seem like the sheriff here might resent you finding something that the county guy missed though?"

Tim nodded.

"So, maybe you shouldn't do that anymore. You know, just to get along with everyone," she suggested, drawing vertical lines in the condensation on her glass.

"I can't help it, and I don't want to stop searching. I owe it to them," Tim said quietly, chewing his bite of duck thoroughly.

"Owe what? And to whom?" his wife challenged, giving him pause.

"The truth, to the deceased. Why are you upset about this?" he blinked at her.

"I just...want us to fit in here. I mean, let's be real, we're a couple of odd ducks, we can't exactly afford to have high profile people looking at us funny, you know?" her tone softened.

"People have always looked at me funny."

"Yeah, me too. But can't you just keep your "stories" to yourself?"

"If someone did some horrible thing to you, would you want the one person who knew about it to stay quiet?"

"Sometimes that's what has to happen in polite society."

"I'm not polite," Tim tossed his fork onto his plate, unable to eat another bite.

"So I noticed," Susannah muttered, itching to get down to her workshop.

CHAPTER 24

"Susannah, I need to talk to you," Tim announced at the breakfast table.

His wife poked the yolk of her egg, taking little satisfaction in seeing the yellow pool oozing toward her potatoes.

"Well, I'm here," she replied, pulling off a chunk of biscuit and dipping it into the goo.

"Have you said anything to anyone about…Rosa's dog?"

"I told Tanner," she popped the biscuit in her mouth and followed it with a swig of strong black coffee.

"We agreed that it was a one-time thing to help your

friend and that that would be the end of it," his mouth worked in frustration. "Who is Tanner?"

"Tanner works with me at the restaurant. He's a new prep cook," she speared a cube of potato.

"Why did you think that it would be okay to tell your new prep cook about...Rosa's dog?" Tim was as astounded as he'd ever been. If things kept going along like this, he might actually raise his voice.

"Don't worry, it's okay. He works with that jerk of a vet, Dr. Dobbins, and sees how he lets animals suffer."

"I never knew that you were an animal lover," Tim said carefully, eyes narrowed.

"What are you trying to say, Timothy?" she challenged.

"Dr. Dobbins said that he'd run into you at the restaurant. He came by to visit me, and I didn't like it. I can't help but wonder how and why you've interacted with him at all, and why that would lead you to confide in your new coworker."

"He's just a kid, don't worry about it. And don't

worry about Doctor Strange either. The only reason that I talked to him is because he enjoyed one of the dishes that I prepared, and they made me go out in the dining room so that he could thank me."

Tim thought for a moment, staring at her.

"That must've been awkward."

"Yeah, it really was. I gotta go. Stop worrying so much about everything, it'll give you wrinkles," she got up from the table and ran a hand over his cheek. "And you've got such nice skin, that would be a shame."

Tim was beyond frustrated, and intended to voice a very strong opinion to his wife after work. He'd had two cat owners and a dog owner stop by, inquiring about his "services." He'd turned them away, after much persuasion, but the last one had threatened to expose him if he didn't help her out. Just like Elmo's owner had. They all said the same thing, they'd found out about him from the young man at the vet clinic, and they knew that Tim had assisted other pet owners.

He sat at his desk, brooding. While he was no animal lover, he had a respect for life that was nearly as deep as his respect for the dead, and the thought of exterminating household pets nauseated him. He wondered how his wife could've had such bad judgment. Why on earth would she have told her coworker what had happened? Perhaps there was something to the hairs on her clothing, perhaps she was having an affair, although he realistically didn't see how that would be possible. For the most part, Susannah hated people. It would be entirely out of character for her to willingly engage in intimacy with someone other than her designated intimacy partner.

While it was true that their relationship was merely cordial most of the time, she'd made it quite clear that she was devoted to him and their relationship, no matter how unconventional it might be. There had been occasions lately where she'd seemed sexually aggressive with him, usually after spending a great deal of time in the basement doing her artwork. He'd made a point to never disturb her when she was down there, but perhaps he should try to learn more about her by watching her create.

Tim found it odd that Susannah would create art,

because visual appeal seemed to be something that didn't really interest her in other areas of life. She wore no makeup, and had a plain haircut. Her clothes were utilitarian, and she didn't decorate the house, but she'd disappear into the basement for hours to work on her projects. If art was so important to her, he should probably make more of an effort to understand her creativity. He'd visit her tonight if she went into her workshop. Maybe he could gain some insight into why she was having conversations with Tanner rather than him.

"I'm going down to the basement for a while, don't wait up," Susannah said, clearing her dinner dishes from the table. "It's your turn to load the dishwasher," she reminded him pleasantly enough.

"Okay," he nodded, still enjoying his food. She'd made an outstanding lasagna, with garlic bread and a green salad, and despite the fact that he was already full, he kept eating, secure in the knowledge that there was a full bottle of antacids in his night stand.

Susannah grabbed a sweater, and headed for the basement. He watched her go, chewing thoughtfully, and decided to join her after he finished the dishes. When he opened the dishwasher, he discovered that his wife hadn't put away the clean dishes from yesterday, so he had to do that before he could load it up again. He put the dishes and leftover food away, scraped the scraps into the disposal and neatly arranged the plates, utensils and glasses in the dishwasher. Wiping his hands on a towel afterwards, he pushed his glasses up his nose, donned a hooded sweatshirt to ward off the chill, and opened the basement door, hearing nothing. The light was on, so he figured that Susannah must be in one of the back rooms, and trotted down the stairs, ready to see and understand the world of her art.

"Suze?" he called out. No answer.

She wasn't in the main room, so he checked the room where she kept her tree. He noticed that there were more leaves on it, and of different colors and textures, but she wasn't in the tree room either. There was a hum from her dehydrator in the corner, and when he peeked inside, he could see small pieces of material that looked like leather drying inside. He opened a cupboard over her workbench and saw various materials that she obviously used in her art. Jars of what looked like ashes, clumps of stuff that looked like she'd shaved the hair from a child's doll, and various oddly shaped bleached out twigs. It was semi dark in the tree room, and he wondered how she worked in there without proper lighting.

Tim left the tree room and saw his wife entering the basement from the storm door which led to the outside.

"What are you doing down here?" she asked, seeming startled.

"I came down to watch you work, but you weren't here," he looked at her pointedly. "What's that?" he asked, gesturing to a black plastic bag in her hand.

"Leaves," she said quickly. "I wanted to add some color to my work, so I collected a bunch of colorful leaves."

"I would've gone with you if you had asked me to," he said gently.

"You would've...been bored," she shrugged, looking away.

"Not if you talked to me," her husband cocked his

head, wondering why Susannah was acting so strangely.

"Well, I appreciate it, but I'd really like to be alone right now, if you don't mind," she still wouldn't meet his eyes.

"I don't mind. I'll see you in a bit."

He went upstairs and got ready for bed, watching TV in his pajamas until his eyes wouldn't stay open any longer. Susannah was still in the basement, and hadn't come up to invite him to join her, so he assumed that she was enjoying her solitude and went to bed. Alone. Again.

The phone on Tim's desk rang the moment that he unlocked the front door of the mortuary and he sprinted across the foyer and into his office to answer it.

"Eckels Mortuary," he said, out of breath.

Sheriff Bemis's voice was definitely not the first thing that he wanted to hear.

"Get your meat wagon down to the morgue. We got a body for ya, and you better do a damn good job on this one," Arlen growled.

"I always do a good job," Tim remarked mildly.

"Yeah, yeah, whatever. Get down there and make the pickup, smartass. The family will be in later today to make the arrangements, but you can get started on doing whatever weirdness you do."

"No, actually I need to know the wishes of the family and have their consent before I proceed."

"Not in Pellman you don't, boy."

Tim sighed, knowing that it was pointless to argue with the belligerent sheriff.

"I'll be right there," he promised.

Tim laid the black bag that was pitifully light onto his table, and unzipped it, reeling at what he saw. The girl's soft, wavy, red hair was the same color and texture of the mass of material that he'd seen in his wife's cupboard in the basement. Or was it? How could it be? It couldn't be…it was just a strange coincidence. He was jumping at shadows and that was not like him. Taking a deep breath, and patting down the hair on the back of his neck, he unzipped the bag the rest of the way.

The girl's eyelids were missing, so he'd have to construct new ones, which wasn't as difficult as it sounded, but attaching new eyebrows and eyelashes would be tedious. Clearly this was the victim that the sheriff had come to see him about, because so far, things were looking very suspicious. He started his examination as he always did, by taking photos, from head to toe. The challenge this corpse presented with her lack of eyelashes and eyebrows might just win him space in Mortuary Monthly if he did a spectacular job.

When Tim got down to the girl's feet, he slowly lowered the camera and leaned over for a closer look. On the top of the girl's foot, there was a patch of skin missing. A patch of skin that was in the exact shape of…a leaf. Overcome as his system flooded with terror, Tim ran to the nearest industrial sink and spewed his breakfast into the drain. He wasn't grossed out, not by a long shot, it took far more than a missing patch of skin to make Timothy Eckels turn green. He'd never thrown up after seeing a body, even when the body had been that of his beloved Gram. No, what made the mortician sick was the dead certainty that he was married to a monster who made art from human flesh.

Abigail Sorenson wasn't the first, he realized with dread. He'd run into at least two other victims with similar patches of skin, and hair and various other body parts missing. Could his mild-mannered mate actually be a serial killer? A wave of revulsion swept through Tim, and he held onto the sink as his body shuddered and shook. The mortician had the utmost respect for remains, but utter disdain for those who created them before their time. Body preparation was an art form, but killing bodies to make art was just simply…murder. Cold, hard, merciless murder.

When his shudders subsided a bit, another blood-chilling thought occurred to him…what if he was next? Why hadn't she killed him yet? He'd seen a look in her eyes that had disturbed him, but he'd shrugged it off, and now she knew that he'd explored her underground workshop of horror. He'd have to be very careful from now on, walking on eggshells around his wife, while desperately searching for evidence that would exonerate her. What would he do if she went to prison? At least he'd be free from the fear that consumed him right now. Feeling intensely disloyal, Tim tried his very best to convince himself that this must all just be coincidental. He'd do a little more exploring, at times when he knew that Susannah was at work and wouldn't interrupt his search.

In the meantime, he had a body to prepare, which needed extensive work in order to appear like the fresh-face young woman who'd been smothered was merely asleep. Tim was wracked with constant anxiety as he finished taking his photos. He reconstructed the murder of Abigail, picturing his wife calmly dissecting her after her life had been snuffed out. He knew that duct tape had been used to suffocate her, he saw the sticky remnants on her face. The coroner had obviously removed the tape, but spots of adhesive still clung to her cold discolored cheeks.

The mortician felt so wrung out by the time that he'd taken the photos and stitched up the wound on her foot, and the missing patch from her scalp, that he closed down for the day, tucking the girl neatly into a refrigerated drawer. He planned to do the reconstruction of her eyelids tomorrow, after he'd had a chance to rest. Perhaps the shaking in his hands might stop by then. Tim leaned against the bank of refrigerated drawers after closing Abigail's, and closed his eyes, frazzled and weary.

"Rough day?" Susannah's voice made him jump, his heart threatening to leap from his chest.

He took a deep, shaky breath.

"It always is when I have to deal with the sheriff," he hedged.

"The sheriff? Again?" Susannah raised an eyebrow. "What did he want?"

"To make sure that I did a good job on my latest deceased," the mortician shrugged, avoiding his wife's eyes.

"Why would he care?"

"Who knows? Maybe he knew the family. Pellman is a small town."

"Did he say anything else?" she asked, appearing nonchalant, but for the tightness around her mouth.

"Thankfully, no. I'm always glad to see him leave," Tim admitted truthfully.

"I brought home dinner. Coq au Vin, if you're hungry."

Tim's stomach rolled and flopped at the thought of putting anything in his mouth that had been prepared by the hands that had cut pieces from a pretty teenager. Bile rose again in his throat, and he swallowed hard against it.

"Actually, I think I may be coming down with something. I'm not feeling well," he placed a hand on his stomach and grimaced.

Susannah stepped back. She might be a serial killer, but she was also more than paranoid about coming into contact with germs.

"Should I put sheets on the bed in the guest room for you?" she asked.

"That would be quite nice," Tim nodded, relieved that at least he wouldn't have to lie beside her.

While he was trying to convince himself that there was no possible way that his wife could be a serial killer, he wasn't quite there yet, so staying away from her was a more comfortable option for now.

"Okay, see you at home," she turned and headed for the stairs.

"I'll be there shortly," he said, his breath coming in shallow gasps.

As Susannah turned away, he spotted something on the sole of her shoe that looked suspiciously like blood.

CHAPTER 25

Dr. Bradley Dobbins looked at his appointments for the day, and noticed that something seemed to be missing.

"Jenna," he got his spunky blonde receptionist's attention. "Isn't Thursday when Elmo is supposed to come in for his treatment?"

"Hang on a sec," she tapped on the computer. "Yep, Thursdays are his treatment days, but there's a note in here that says he's missing," she turned to face him with a confused frown.

"Missing?" the vet's eyes darkened.

"Yep, they've been looking for him since last Friday."

"The day after his last treatment."

"Looks that way."

"Get his owner on the phone, see if they have any idea as to where he might be."

"Okay," Jenna stared at her boss's retreating back, wondering at his strange reaction to the news that Elmo was missing.

Bradley threw down his appointment list in disgust. He had quotas to meet, and losing pets was costing him money. Up until a couple of months ago, he'd been engaging in a regular cycle of giving the pets a little something to create symptoms, then treating them to make the symptoms go away with his magical supplements. It was working out quite well, and the bonuses that he was getting from the pharmaceutical company had gone a long way toward making his dream of retiring in the Caribbean a reality.

Elmo wasn't the first. A scraggly cat named Bootsie had disappeared, as had an ill-tempered mutt named Victor. When Dobbins gave Victor his "bad dose," he'd gone ahead and made him a little sicker than usual, simply because the beast had tried to bite him, and, failing in that, had peed on his lab coat. Three revenue streams had just up and disappeared, and Brad didn't believe for an instant that it was merely a coincidence. He had to get to the bottom of this mess, and soon, before it wiped out his hopes for retiring well.

Jenna tapped timidly at his office door, but smiled the coy smile that had made him hire her on the spot, despite the fact that she'd had no veterinary training or experience.

"Dr. Dobbins, they said that they have no idea where Elmo might be, and that they're heart broken."

Bradley sighed and nodded.

"Fine. Let them know that I can put them in touch with a good breeder when they're ready, and that sooner is better than later. They need to put their grief behind them by caring for another animal."

"I'll let them know," Jenna agreed, sending him another soft smile that caused him to stir a bit, in spite of his bad mood.

"I have an emergency situation that I need to tend to, so I'll be gone for an hour or two. Reschedule whatever appointments you need to," he instructed as she left.

"Will do. I hope everything's okay."

"It will be."

Sheriff Arlen Bemis regarded the clearly enraged veterinarian on the other side of the desk, hands tented under his chin.

"I'm telling you, Arlen, it's gotta be that mortician who's behind all of this. I didn't have any issues with pets dying until he came and set up shop. Now I've had three disappear in less than two months," Brad insisted.

"Could be coincidence," the sheriff mused, not rattled in the least.

"But it's not. Mrs. Truman saw that evil mutt Victor going into the mortuary."

"Maybe Victor's owner is one of those people who takes their dog everywhere."

"I can assure you, Rosa does not take her dog everywhere with her. She works in food service for crying out loud. Restaurants are pretty picky about dog hair in the food," Brad sneered. "Wait! That's it," he snapped his fingers, his eyes manic.

"What?" Arlen sighed.

"Rosa worked at Le Chateau. Guess who else works at Le Chateau??" the veterinarian exclaimed excitedly.

"Elmo's mom?" the sheriff rolled his eyes.

"No! The mortician's wife. She's one of the chefs. Don't you see...she probably told Rosa that her husband would kill Victor for her, so she could stop paying her vet bills."

"Bit of a stretch, don't you think?"

"No, Arlen, I don't think it's a stretch, I think this animal-loving mortician with a conscience is ruining my business, and I want it to stop now. He's not licensed to euthanize, which is a crime."

"A crime for which there is absolutely no evidence," the sheriff reminded the agitated vet.

"And what about that young girl who died? What if he was involved with that?"

"He had an alibi, and the evidence, once again, doesn't put him anywhere near that girl or the crime. If you want me to go after this guy, the evidence has to back you up, otherwise it's nothing but wild speculation."

"Oh, there'll be plenty of evidence when I get done with Eckels," Bradley finally relaxed a bit, the corner of his mouth curling into a rather unpleasant smirk.

"This sounds like something that I don't want to hear," Arlen remarked, standing. "You got time for lunch?"

Dobbins glanced at his watch. It wouldn't hurt his patients to keep them waiting for another hour, it's not like they were going to die.

"Of course I do," he agreed. Lunch would be a celebration of sorts, because he intended to put his newly-conceived plan into action upon his return.

"Tanner, I'd like a word with you, please," Dobbins

informed his glorified kennel attendant when he returned to the clinic.

"Uh…okay," the young man agreed, following him back to his office.

"Please, sit down," Brad gestured to a chair in front of his desk, and instead of sitting across the desk in his leather executive chair, took a seat across from the clearly nervous lad.

Tanner crossed his feet at the ankles, his bony arms resting on the arms of the chair, and looked at the vet with a mixture of suspicion and what looked like fear.

"Do you like working here?" Brad asked, perversely enjoying the young man's discomfort.

"Why? Did I do something wrong?" he peered out from under the hair that swooped over and covered one eye almost completely.

"No, no, of course not, I'm just asking you if you enjoy working here."

"Uh…yeah, I do."

"Why?"

"Well, it's easy, and I like the animals," Tanner shrugged.

"Sounds like we're paying you too much," Dobbins chuckled.

"I...uh..." the young man didn't know how to respond.

"Don't worry, I was kidding," the vet let him off the hook with a practiced smile. "However, if you'd like a chance to earn some extra money, I might know of a way to make that happen."

"Umm...yeah, I could use more money. Are you going to increase my hours? I have another part time job, and..."

Dobbins held up a hand, stopping the young man's questions.

"Even better. You can keep your other job, and do something else during the times that you'd normally be here."

"Something else?"

"Yes. I would supplement whatever your new employer pays you."

"But…why would you do that?" Tanner frowned.

"Because I need something that you can get for me."

"What's that?"

"Information. You interested? I'll make it worth your while."

"Yes, sir," the young man nodded, intrigued.

CHAPTER 26

Tanner Benson had dressed in his best jeans, a short-sleeved white dress shirt, and the only tie that he owned, a purple paisley left over from when he'd attended his father's funeral. His long thin hair was pulled back into what he hoped was a respectable pony tail, and he'd shaved the scattered wisps of hair on his chin, so that he looked fresh-faced for the interview that he hoped to have.

He didn't know why Bradley Dobbins wanted so badly for him to work with Susannah's husband, but he was willing to let Tanner keep his job at the vet clinic, as well as pay him extra for working with the mortician. With three jobs instead of two, he might be able to start taking some classes at the local community college. Even if they were online, he'd at least be able to knock out some of his core requirements.

"You're not returning the dog," Tim stated flatly when he came upstairs and saw Tanner loitering in the foyer of the funeral home.

"Uh…no, I'm not. He's a good boy," the young man fought the urge to jam his hands into his pockets or cross his arms. He wanted to make a good impression and body language was important.

"Then what is it that you need?" the stressed-out mortician sighed. He'd been working all morning on Abigail Sorenson's eyelashes, and his neck hurt from craning closer to his task lamp in order to make precise adjustments.

"Uh…so, when I was here the other day, I saw…what you were working on, and I, uh…would really like to learn to do that."

"Then go to school," Tim replied dismissively, turning to go.

"Wait," Tanner said, panicking a bit. "I was thinking that, since you're really busy here…maybe I could do some things that you don't like to do. You know, so that you can just do the stuff that you wanna do. And then…if there's any time after I do whatever you need, maybe you could teach me the other stuff…the interesting stuff. You know, like an apprentice," he proposed, his eyes wide and guileless.

The truth was, he did want to know more about what Tim did. It seemed to him to be very similar to his hobby, but with people instead of animals. It didn't matter in his mind, that, while he actually was truly interested in mortuary science, he was mostly interested in the money to be gained from becoming Tim's apprentice.

Tim paused for a moment, appearing to consider the proposition.

"I'm not good with people," he muttered.

"I could talk to people for you if you wanted me to," Tanner offered, hating the idea, but wanting the job.

Tim stared at him, blinking, and the door opened, admitting an elderly woman who walked with a cane.

"Well Tanner, it's lovely to see you here," she smiled, making a beeline for the two men. "You're not here for a loved one, are you?"

"How are you Mrs. Parsons?" the young man smiled.
"No, I'm just here talking to Mr. Eckels about a job."

"Well, how lovely. You're not leaving Dr. Dobbins though, are you?"

"No ma'am, I'll still be there."

"That's good. Fluffy responds so well to you. That's why I'm here. I'm following your advice," she leaned forward and whispered, patting Tanner's arm.

Tim was more than irritated that apparently, another person was coming to him for the compassionate euthanizing of their pet. Before he could say anything, however, Tanner stepped in to save the day.

"Oh, yeah, I'm sorry, but I made a mistake. I thought it was Mr. Eckels who...you know, but it wasn't. The guy who owned this place before him did that," the young man lied.

"Virgil? That shocks me to my foundations. No wonder he moved out of town, his mama would not have approved. Okay," Mrs. Parsons nodded sadly. "I guess I'll just keep treating Fluffy and see what happens. I just hate seeing her suffer."

"Me too," Tanner agreed, walking her to the door. "All we can do is hope for the best."

"All right dear. Thank you so much," she waved and shuffled out the door.

"You're hired," Tim said tonelessly.

Tanner had actually enjoyed his time at the mortuary, taking care of families who came in to pick out caskets or select funeral plans, and, at the end of the day, watching Tim work on restoring a healthy glow to the corpse of Abigail Sorenson. It was peaceful, and the way that Timothy Eckels worked with the deceased seemed almost to be a tribute of sorts. It had been a long day, but the work wasn't rocket science, so, while he was tired, he still felt good.

Arriving home, he saw a black plastic trash bag, which clearly had something small in it, snugged up to his front door. He grabbed it by the cinch ties and took it inside with him. Once he'd laid it on his tiny dinette table, he read the tag that was attached to it:

I saw this today and thought that you might be able to make it into something. SE

Curious, he opened up the garbage bag, and was horrified to find a fat grey tabby cat lying stiffly in a pool of blood. The poor thing's fur was saturated with it and, turning it over, Tanner saw that the source of the blood was a stab wound to the neck. There were some claw marks in the bag which led him to believe that the otherwise healthy looking cat had been alive when it was placed inside, and had tried to fight its way out.

He stroked the top of the cat's head, noticing the brilliant gold of his eyes, despite the clouding of death.

"I'm sorry little guy," he murmured. "I'll take care of you, I promise."

Since he had to get ready for his dinner shift at Le Chateau, Tanner left the cat in the bag and placed him in the freezer so that he could deal with him later. He washed his hands, changed into his chef pants and jacket, and headed for the door.

"How'd you like it?" Susannah asked with a secretive smile when Tanner came into the kitchen of Le Chateau.

"Did you kill it?" he asked, his expression guarded.

Her smile vanished, and her eyes darted a bit before she answered.

"No, of course not. I found it and just thought that you might want to do something with it," she shrugged. "If you don't like it, I can take it to my husband so that he can torch it."

"No, I'll make something with it," Tanner replied, hiding his disgust.

"I have some trout to fillet if you'd like," she offered.

"No, I'll just do the squash," he murmured, turning away.

CHAPTER 27

Bradley Dobbins sat in his living room, staring into space, brooding. He didn't know why he was so convinced that the weasel of an undertaker was undermining his business, but the timing seemed more than coincidental, and he sort of had a witness who saw a dog going in to the mortuary. A dog who just happened to disappear from his treatment program. He'd worked too damn hard to let some creepy mortician with a conscience ruin everything. The pasty, paunchy, bespectacled man didn't seem terribly bright, which made it even more important for Brad to defeat him.

He'd given the weird new vet tech a hundred bucks to try to get hired on so that he'd have someone on the inside over at the mortuary, and while he didn't know how trustworthy the young hipster was, it certainly seemed like his loyalty could be bought. He'd get daily reports from the guy, and either the kid would find something incriminating, or the vet would have to take matters into his own hands. He rather relished the idea of setting the mild-mannered mortician up, but for now, he'd bide his time.

Bradley's cat still hadn't come back, and his paranoia whispered that it had to have been Tim who'd come and taken the animal. Inexplicably, a chill crept down the veterinarian's spine as he sat in his chair in the darkened living room. He hadn't heard or seen anything out of the ordinary, but he had the strange sensation that he was no longer alone. He sat up straighter in his chair, listening, waiting, and just as he was about to turn around, he was caught up in a chokehold.

It was the oddest thing, the arm that circled his neck was thick and strong, yet smelled somehow feminine. He remembered thinking that perhaps he wasn't Tim's first victim of the evening. Perhaps there had been a woman who died first.

Susannah had been frustrated at Tanner's reaction to her gift, very frustrated. Perhaps she'd misjudged him. She'd thought that he'd been much like she had as a younger woman, but that was probably wishful thinking. How crazy was it that she thought she might finally have found a human being who actually understood her. No one understood her...ever. Part of her reluctance to kill her husband was the fact that, while he didn't know about her "interesting" hobby, and couldn't even begin to understand her, he seemed to accept her, for better or worse. That was something that she'd never experienced before, and she was in no hurry to give it up. Hopefully he hadn't seen anything when he visited the basement that made him suspicious, she'd really hate to have to end him.

Now, Tanner, on the other hand...if he even suspected what she did for fun, he'd have to be eliminated. She'd enjoyed his company for a period of time, but if he couldn't be trusted, she had ways of taking care of such issues. She wouldn't let him experience terror, and would make sure that he felt no pain if she had to kill him, but she would do it without a second thought if she deemed it necessary.

The more she thought about how stupid she'd been in trusting another human, even slightly, the angrier she became at herself. She knew better. She couldn't afford the luxury of friends. People were selfish, people had agendas, people didn't understand. They never had and they never would. She chopped and seared and diced and sautéed, working herself into a frenzy, so that, by the time she left Le Chateau, she had to do something to blow off some steam, or she'd just snap. She didn't want to accidentally kill her husband because she was worked up.

Dr. Dobbins' time hadn't yet arrived, but that didn't mean that she couldn't toy with him for a bit. She'd slip into her basement, change into her "play" clothes, and pay him a visit that he wouldn't forget. She wanted to feel his racing heart against her body, wanted to smell and taste his fear. She wanted to make him beg for mercy, and then she'd slip out into the night, to return another day.

Susannah dearly loved chloroform, and the fact that it was so easy to get on the internet. She particularly loved to use it when surprising a male who was bigger and/or stronger than she was, because the thrill of clamping it tightly over their nose and mouth while they struggled and fought, the whites of their eyes revealing their terror, gave her a tremendous rush of adrenalin, and an almost god-like sense of power. When they finally succumbed, she could do with them as she pleased.

Bradley Dobbins was mildly fit. He went to the gym a few times a week to run on the treadmill, or ride an exercise bike while he caught up on email and social media. He did little to develop his muscles and upper body strength, however, which meant that, though he had a bit of stamina, his struggles were no match for the powerfully-built woman who held him from behind. Susannah smiled behind her nylon ski mask, content to know that Dobbins had neither seen her face, nor guessed her identity.

She wanted to humiliate the arrogant veterinarian, as well as terrify him, so once he had fallen into a deep, chloroform-induced sleep, she turned him over, and eased his workout pants down below his buttocks. Taking out her scalpel, she scored perhaps the most satisfying leaves of the Fall season.

"Sit on this Dr. Dobbins," she murmured with a smile, tucking her latest trophies into a plastic bag.

The vet's blood had made quite a mess on his Persian rug, which was a shame, the rug was quite lovely and undoubtedly valuable, but Susannah shook off that pesky bit of remorse. From Bradley's medicine cabinet she took a roll of gauze and some surgical tape, binding his fresh wounds to minimize damage to the carpet, and left him lying there, face down, with a bandage on each cheek, giving new meaning to the phrase "butt-hurt."

With adrenalin still tingling her nerve endings, she left the McMansion feeling much better. It hadn't been a kill, but she'd put an obnoxious jerk in his place, and delighted at the thought that he'd be jumping at shadows for weeks after this incident. She loved that he'd be paranoid now, loved that he'd be scared and angry and carry his negative emotions around with him like a festering disease. Even though it'd make eventually killing him more difficult, now that he'd be watchful, she chuckled, knowing that she was in control, she called all the shots, she decided whether he lived or died, and whether he'd be able to sit comfortably. He thought that he held the power, and perhaps over innocent animals, he did, but she held the power over him, and that was the thought that kept her warm as she slipped out of the gated community and into the night.

CHAPTER 28

Tanner stood beside Tim, watching raptly as the mortician placed plastic caps under Abigail Sorenson's newly crafted eyelids, so that her eyes wouldn't appear sunken.

"Do you do that for everyone?" he asked quietly, not wanting to disturb his somewhat taciturn boss.

"Anyone who is having a viewing. Family members find sunken eyes to be rather disconcerting," he commented dryly, moving on to the next eye.

"She looks like she's just sleeping."

"That's the goal. This way they can remember her as she was."

"You're actually an artist," the young man remarked.

Tim, always uncomfortable with compliments, let that one pass.

"I do art too," Tanner offered, again getting no response from his introverted boss. "I can bring something in to show you sometime."

"If you'd like," Tim muttered, hoping that his reply would make his assistant stop talking.

"Can I do anything to help?"

"Cut off a two foot length of that black thread, and hand me that packet of sterilized needles," Tim gestured with his head, while gently closing Abigail's eyelid.

"Okay," Tanner nodded, glad to be allowed to participate, even in a small way. "What's it for?"

"Mouth work is next."

"Oh." The young man swallowed, wondering what that might mean, then glanced at his watch, irritated to see that it was time to head to Le Chateau for the dinner hour. "I gotta go."

"Okay," was the distracted reply, as the mortician

threaded his needle.

Tanner trotted up the stairs, only to come charging right back down.

"Mr. Eckels, sorry to bother you, but the sheriff is on his way in, and he doesn't look happy.

Tim sighed and pulled his needle through Abigail's fragile flesh, holding it up in the air and staring at his assistant.

"Alright, when you see him on your way out, tell him I'll be right up," the mortician frowned.

If he never saw Arlen Bemis again, it would be too soon. He carefully laid the needle down on the table next to Abigail's head, snapped off his rubber gloves, and trudged up the stairs to find a decidedly agitated sheriff pacing the foyer.

"You've gone too far this time, Eckels," Bemis said, without preamble. "I was willing to pass Brad's rantings off as paranoia, but this time you've gone too far. I don't know how you did it, I don't know why you did it, but I'm gonna nail you to the wall on this one, you sick bastard," he fumed.

"As usual, Sheriff, I have no idea what you're talking about," Tim sighed.

"It's hard for newcomers to fit in sometimes, but most folks usually try. You never did. You don't go out, you don't meet people, you're weird and quiet and maybe that's just the way that you keep people at a distance. And why would you want to do that, I wonder?"

"Is being an introvert a crime these days?" the mortician quipped, pushing his coke bottle glasses up his nose.

"Don't get smart with me boy, you've got some explaining to do, and you better start talkin," Arlen ordered.

"Anything in particular that you want me to talk about?"

"You can start with explaining where the hell you were, and what you were doing about nine o'clock last night."

Tim thought for a moment. He'd been staying away from home because he wasn't quite ready to sit in the same room with Susannah for any length of time, and he wondered if what the sheriff wanted to talk with him about had anything to do with what he suspected was his wife's hobby.

"I was at Billy Brew at nine o'clock."

"What were you doing there? You don't strike me as the type of guy who hangs out at a bar," the sheriff raised a skeptical brow.

"I went there for dinner, and after dinner I had dessert and then I stayed for a while to watch some television. There was a marathon on of my favorite true crime show."

"Lemme get this straight…your wife is a frickin' chef at a four-star restaurant, and you went to Billy Brew for dinner? Can you prove that you were there?"

"I have the receipt in my wallet. They usually put time stamps on such things," the mortician reached for his wallet, opened it, flipped through half a dozen receipts, and found the one from Billy Brew, handing it to the sheriff.

"Where did you go after this," Arlen growled, seeing the time stamp that said 10:30.

"I went to the grocery store and did some shopping, then I went home."

"I'm sure you have the receipt for that too."

"Of course, I always keep them until I can record them," Tim replied, innocently, which seemed to infuriate the sheriff. He pulled out the grocery receipt and handed it over.

"Who the hell is that organized?" Arlen muttered, looking at the receipt.

"I am," the mortician shrugged.

"Shut up, Eckels. I've had just about enough of that mouth," the sheriff glared at him, tucking both receipts into his shirt pocket. He looked as though he was about to follow up his rude directive with a comment when suddenly he fixated on something behind the mortician.

"What the hell is that?" he growled, pushing past Tim and heading for a pew-like bench that graced one wall of the foyer. Once there, he picked up a garment and held it carefully. "Whose is this?" he demanded.

Tim raised his eyebrows.

"I have no idea."

"Is it yours?"

"No."

"I'm taking it into evidence."

"Evidence? Evidence of what?" Tim was baffled.

"What kind of relationship do you have with Dr. Bradley Dobbins?"

"I don't have any kind of relationship with him. We only met once, when he came in here."

"Why did he do that?"

"Because he ran into my wife at Le Chateau."

"Uh-huh," the sheriff stared him down. "If this is what I think it is…you're in big trouble, Eckels. Don't even think about leaving town or I'll hunt you down and throw you in jail myself, you hear? You're a person of interest in the assault of Dr. Dobbins and the murders of Abigail Sorenson and Jorge Hernandez."

The sheriff turned on his heel and left, leaving Tim staring after him. He loved his wife, in his own way, but he wasn't willing to go to prison to protect her, wasn't willing to take the fall for her heinous hobby. He had to find out if his Susannah was really a cold-blooded killer, or if her strange hobby was just that. The leaves on her tree could be made from leather, or tissue paper, or any number of things...but he had to find out for sure, and hoped that he didn't become the next victim in the process.

CHAPTER 29

"Timmy, have you seen my jacket?" Susannah called, digging in the hamper as though her life depended upon it.

"What does it look like?" he trailed down the hall, with a mug of hot tea in his hand, fearing that he knew how she would answer.

"It looks like a jacket. It's dark brown nylon, kind of silky-feeling…" she said, closing the hamper and heading for the bedroom.

Tim's heart thumped against his chest. He knew he had to act completely normal. He had to act as if he didn't know that the missing jacket was sitting in an evidence room.

"Doesn't sound familiar. When did you have it last? Could you have left it at work?"

"No, I didn't wear it to work. I may have left it in the mortuary when I went over to help you with the books, are you sure you didn't see it in your office?"

Tim shook his head, trying desperately to hide the shaking in his hands by wrapping them around his tea mug, as though for warmth, but nothing could dissipate the chill that was currently crawling up his spine.

"No, I haven't seen it. I'll have to ask Tanner if he saw it."

Susannah's frantic motion stopped, and she slowly turned to stare at her husband.

"Tanner?" she asked, her voice dropping a couple of octaves. She drilled him with her gaze, clearly waiting for an explanation.

"Yes, he started working for me this week. Now he works with both of us," Tim attempted to smile, his face feeling foreign.

"Why did you hire someone? We didn't discuss this," she demanded, her voice low.

"I didn't know that you'd want to be a part of that decision. He does the things that I don't like to do."

"Like what?" her eyes narrowed.

"Like talking to people, helping them with their funeral plans, casket selection, that kind of thing. He also vacuums and takes out the trash," Tim shrugged. "I didn't think you'd have any reason to be involved in the hiring process."

"How did you find him?"

"Uh...what?" Tim tried to buy some time, wondering why Susannah was making such a big deal out of this.

"How. Did. You. Find. Him?" she snipped moving closer with every word, until she was past his comfort zone, her face only a couple of feet from his.

A brief, horrific image of her stabbing him to death in his sleep flashed before his eyes, and he pretended to cough for a moment so that he could get his panic under control.

"Sorry," he replied, breathless. "Allergies. I didn't find him, he came in and asked for a job."

"And you gave him one," she spat the accusation.

"Yes."

"Did you bother to interview him? Or run a background check?"

"No, I…" Tim began.

"You let a stranger off the street just waltz right in and start working with you, representing your company, when you don't know anything about him."

"He works with you and you don't mind. You made it sound like you talk to him more than you talk to me," the hurt and scared husband stated quietly.

"Is that what you think?" she seemed taken aback.

Tim shrugged, gazing at the floor, uncomfortable.

"I'm sorry if I've been distant, and I'm sorry if I spoke too harshly, but do you have any idea who Tanner works for?"

"Andre?"

"No, besides Andre. Tanner works for Bradley Dobbins, the vet."

The hairs on the back of Tim's neck stood up and things suddenly came sharply into focus. Of course it hadn't been his hard-working wife who had killed two people and assaulted the veterinarian, it had to have been his new assistant. His relief was profound. Susannah's leaves were probably just leaves, and it hadn't been her who had taken patches of skins from the bodies that he'd prepared recently.

"That explains a lot," he said mildly. "He must be telling the vet things that he sees here."

"What do you mean?" she sounded alarmed.

"For some reason, the vet keeps accusing me of things. He somehow knew about the two pets that I... dealt with, and thinks that I'm out to get him. Someone attacked him last night and he swears it was me. It must've been Tanner."

"The vet blames you?" Susannah murmured. "Interesting."

"I know, it's ridiculous," Tim nodded. "Want some ice cream?"

"You must be feeling better," his wife remarked.

"Much better."

"Let's go get ice cream then," she smiled a strange smile and hooked her arm through his.

Bradley Dobbins leaned over on one hip, unable to rest his weight on the sutured areas of his lower buttocks, and casually asked Tanner about his time with Timothy Eckels.

"Well, I mean, I'm not exactly a party animal," the young man shrugged, looking mildly embarrassed. "But his life is so totally boring. He doesn't talk, he doesn't like being around people, it seems like the only thing that he's into is his work. That's probably why he's so good at it."

"Is he that good at it?" Brad was skeptical, his mouth twisted with derision.

Tanner nodded.

"He's an artist, it's amazing."

"How technical is what he does? Is it challenging? Would it be easy to make a mistake?"

"There's a lot to remember. I don't know how he does

it without a checklist, but I guess he's been doing it for a long time."

"I'd be fascinated to hear how his process works…do you think you could walk me through it sometime?"

"Well, I don't know all that much yet. I can only observe when all my other work is done. Sometimes I'm meeting with people for most of my shift."

"Try to see more…I'm really interested," Dobbins said with a smile.

"Sure. I am too, I get it," Tanner nodded.

"Good then, here's a little something for you. Don't spend it all in one place," he said, handing over a fifty dollar bill.

"I won't. Thanks," the young man felt strange about accepting the money, but was grateful for it.

CHAPTER 30

"I'm sorry, I'll no longer be requiring your services," Timothy Eckels said stiffly when Tanner came in to work.

The young man's eyes grew wide. Not only had he just accepted another payment from Dr. Dobbins, but he was also genuinely fascinated with the work and eager to learn.

"But, why? I looked on the schedule...all of the drawers are full," he commented, referring to the cold storage. "And we have back to back funerals this week."

"No, you're mistaken. I have back to back funerals and full drawers. You have nothing more than a check for services rendered that will be coming in the mail in two to five working days."

"Did I do something wrong? If I did, I can stay late to fix it," Tanner implored. "I'm not scheduled at the restaurant tonight, so I'd be able to help you get ahead on some things."

Tim was surprised at the young man's reaction. His expression was open and honest, and his desire to help seemed real. The mortician paused, staring thoughtfully at his young assistant.

"Why do you want to keep this job so badly?" he asked.

"First, I need the money. I mean, that's why everyone works, right? And second, this is really interesting to me, and I might learn something that will help me with my art projects," Tanner explained, his gaze level.

An inward shudder traveled through Tim, raising the hairs on his neck. Was the young man really admitting that he considered killing and taking trophies from his victims a form of art?

"I brought one of them with me today, if you want to

see it. I thought you might like it," he offered shyly, a deep red blush rising from his neck and reaching to the tips of his ears as he glanced down.

Tim's mind raced. What did the young man mean? Had he brought a victim with him? Surely not. His curiosity outweighing his caution, he nodded and spoke a bit hoarsely.

"Uh, yes, I'd like to see it."

"Really?" Tanner looked up, a half-smile quirking one corner of his mouth, as though suddenly his hope had been restored.

"Yes," the mortician swallowed, dreading what he might see in the next few moments.

"Okay, I'll go get it out of my car."

"Can you manage it by yourself?" Tim's interest was certainly piqued.

Another half-smile from Tanner.

"Yeah, it doesn't weigh very much at all, and I'm hoping that it won't be too messy," he said, heading for the door, entirely unaware that his boss had paled significantly at his word choice.

"Messy?" Tim whispered, watching him go and wondering what he'd soon be seeing.

Snapping on a pair of gloves, just in case, the mortician waited for his assistant to return with his "art project," whatever that might be. It seemed that the young man was only gone an instant, and when Tim heard Tanner's footsteps coming effortlessly down the basement stairs, he worked his face into a mask of impassivity.

Tanner was carrying a large black plastic bag, and asked where he should put it. Tim pointed mutely to his draining table, and followed him over to it. The bag was too small to contain an entire human being, and he tried to visualize what sort of stitched-together abomination might be inside. Unconsciously holding his breath, he watched carefully as the young man set the bag down on the table, and began rolling it down from the top, revealing what was inside. He blinked, confused.

"A cat?" the mortician remarked, nonplussed.

"Isn't he great?" Tanner gazed at the lifeless grey-furred animal with an eerie fondness.

"You do taxidermy."

"Yep, taught myself," was the shyly proud response.

"Your work is flawless," the mortician mused, stepping closer and peering at the cat, who looked as though he'd been flash frozen while leaping to swipe at a toy. The fur was intact, the form was perfect, and the eyes seemed to dance with mischief.

"Thanks," Tanner looked away, but glowed at the praise from his boss.

"Why?"

"Why what?" the young man was confused.

"Why did you choose this as your art?" Tim wasn't put off at all, he was fascinated.

"Because animals are beautiful, and just because they die, doesn't mean that they can't stay beautiful. See, that's why I want to know how to do what you do…I can make animals look like they're still alive, and you make people look like they are. It just seems like a logical progression," he shrugged.

Timothy examined the cat from multiple angles.

"This is really good work," he commented, more to himself than the young man standing at the table.

He turned to stare at Tanner, and his gaze seemed far away.

"Okay," he replied finally. "You can stay. For now."

Sheriff Arlen Bemis slid onto the red pleather upholstery opposite Bradley Dobbins in the corner booth at Herb's Diner, and the look on his face indicated that bad news might be coming.

"Did you finally get something on the mortician?" Dobbins asked, dipping a corner of buttered white toast into the yolk pooled on his plate.

"No, because he didn't do it," the sheriff replied, flagging a server for coffee.

"What are you talking about? Of course he did," the veterinarian insisted through a mouthful of his breakfast.

"I'm sorry Brad, but it just didn't play out that way. We found the pair of shoes that matched the footprints found at the scene of the Sorenson girl's murder, and we arrested the guy."

Dobbins stopped his attack on his food and stared at Bemis, mouth slightly agape.

"What? Who?" he demanded

"The shoes were thrown in a dumpster behind a grocery store. There's a homeless guy who sleeps back there most nights, and when the shoes were picked up, it didn't take a genius to notice that the guy had no shoes on. They were his size and DNA in the shoes matched his DNA. There was trace evidence of the victim's blood on the shoes, and the guy had no alibi. It doesn't get much clearer than that," Arlen shrugged, taking a slug of his coffee.

"It's gotta be a setup," Bradley's eyes narrowed. "Eckels is too smart. He set the guy up. He probably took the shoes, wore them to commit the crime, then threw them away near the homeless guy's spot so they'd be found and the homeless guy would be blamed," he theorized, his eyes taking on a desperate look.

"That theory might hold water, except for one important detail," the sheriff replied, trying to hold on to his patience.

"What detail?" the vet demanded.

"The homeless guy's shoes were a size nine. Eckels wears a ten and a half. There's no way that he would have been able to cram his feet into those shoes, much less wear them on a trek through the woods."

"Maybe he didn't put them on until he got to the crime scene."

Bemis shook his head.

"Nope, our tracking expert traced the path that was taken all the way back to where the perp entered the woods with the victim. He had to have found her while she was walking home from school. The shoe prints were consistent."

"Was he wearing the shoes when he left the body? Were there prints found that led away from the crime scene?"

"Yep, and the shoes were still on his feet."

Dobbins sat back and ran a hand through his hair in frustration.

"There has to be more to this story, I just know it. And this homeless guy can't be the one who attacked me. The person who attacked me smelled clean, like they'd taken a shower and then hugged a woman. Or killed one. I'm going to get to the bottom of this Arlen, and when I do, Eckels is going down," he gritted his teeth.

"Leave it alone, Brad," the sheriff said tiredly. "We've got our guy, and life will be a lot safer in Pellman from now on."

"Have you tied the homeless guy to the other murders?" the veterinarian challenged.

"It's only a matter of time."

CHAPTER 31

Susannah Eckels smiled a predatory smile. The news that a suspected serial killer had been caught, while he slept behind the grocery store, had been splashed all over the morning paper, and was being talked about on the radio and in every barbershop and café all over Pellman. They'd fallen for it, even giving the killer the nickname "The Skinner," which cracked her up. She'd set up the homeless guy as the murderer, and they'd bought it, hook, line and sinker. The clever killer had made certain that, while blood at the crime scene had been minimal, since she'd killed Abigail before taking her art materials, she'd had the foresight to smear just a tad of it on the homeless guy's shoes. His life would probably be better in prison anyway, at least he'd have three square meals a day and access to a shower and clean clothes. Better him than her.

Pondering what she wanted to do about Tanner, whether to kill him or not, Susannah went about her day in a good mood. Not only had she fooled local law enforcement into apprehending an innocent man for her crimes, but now, they'd be relaxed, thinking that there would be no more murders, which would free her up to make more mischief in her quest for new materials.

She was sitting at the kitchen table with the newspaper and her breakfast, when Tim came in and sat down across from her, his bowl of cereal in hand.

"Good morning Timmy," she said, with a satisfied smile, before going back to reading the paper.

"Hi. Can I talk to you for a minute?" he asked, leaving his spoon resting in the cereal.

"Okay." Despite her positive mood, she was always a bit wary when Tim wanted to talk about something.

The mortician was brighter than he appeared, and missed nothing, which made it very difficult to be a serial killer living under his roof.

"I talked to Tanner yesterday..." he began, and the hairs on the back of her neck stood at attention.

"Really? About what?" she interrupted, putting the paper down and suddenly showing an intense interest in her piece of buttered toast with strawberry jam.

"Well, he has this...hobby. He does things with animals."

Susannah stared at him, wondering where he was going with this.

"He does taxidermy, right?" she asked.

"Yes, exactly, and he's really good at it."

"Okay."

"So, I was thinking...I may have been a bit premature in saying no when you asked me about helping people with their animals."

A gleam of interest flickered in her eyes.

"What are you saying, Timmy?" she asked, munching on her toast and hoping that what she thought he meant was actually what he meant.

"I...I think that maybe...I'd be willing to help those pet owners, and if they want to preserve the memory of their pet, I could do what Tanner does."

"You want to learn taxidermy?" Susannah grinned, she couldn't help herself.

"I think it's a fitting way to pay tribute," he blinked at her.

"I couldn't agree more. So you'll...*take care* of people's pets then?"

"In extreme cases, where the animal is suffering, yes," he nodded solemnly.

"Oh Timmy, that's so sweet of you," Susannah reached out impulsively and squeezed his hand, positively giddy.

She looked at his willingness to snuff the animation out of animals as a good start. With any luck, she'd be able to eventually introduce him to the realms in which she lived and breathed. This baby step that her husband was taking might just be the start that he needed to join her in ridding the world of overbearing, ill-mannered, abusive men. If not, perhaps he'd at least be willing to accept her hobby and help her to hide from those who would take exception to it. A "serial killer" had been apprehended, and her mild-mannered husband was taking up euthanasia and taxidermy...it was shaping up to be a banner day.

Susannah was still smiling when she arrived at Le Chateau for the lunch hour. Andre and the prep cooks were already hard at work, and she dovetailed into their fully functioning food production vibe as though she were merely a cog in a well-oiled machine. Tanner was working at the vet clinic today, so she wouldn't be able to share her good news with him yet, but her rosy new outlook had her reconsidering whether or not she'd have to kill him.

The kitchen was running like a dream, and production was flawless until the General Manager came in and whispered in Andre's ear. The Head Chef's face fell, as though he was simultaneously disappointed and horrified. The manager and the chef both glanced at her and continued talking. A feeling of dread began to uncurl in the pit of Susannah's stomach, so she threw herself into her tasks with renewed vigor, knowing that if she looked rattled, whatever suspicions they might have would be easier to confirm. The manager left, and she breathed a silent sigh of relief, that was unfortunately short-lived. After the lunch rush was over, Andre motioned for her to follow him into the office.

"Sit down," he said gravely, sinking into the chair across the desk from her.

"I feel like I've been called to the principal's office," she attempted to joke, but it fell woefully flat. "What's going on?"

Andre looked pained, and stared at the desk for a moment before responding.

"There's been a complaint…" he said finally.

"A complaint? About what?" Susannah frowned. No one had ever, EVER, complained about her food.

"Do you have pets?" the Head Chef asked, inexplicably.

"What?"

"Pets. Do you have pets at home?"

She shook her head. "No, why?"

"It seems as though a dish that you prepared for one of last week's lunches was virtually teeming with animal hair, according to the gentleman who called in the complaint," Andre wrinkled his nose, clearly appalled at the thought.

"That's absurd. I'm not even in contact with animals, there's no way that could have happened, and even if it had, the garnish guys and the servers check this dishes thoroughly before they go out, they would've caught that."

"That was my thought, but now we have this complaint," Andre sighed, frowning.

"When did he complain?" Susannah tried to keep her voice from shaking with anger.

"This morning, I believe."

"He had hair in his lunch last week and he waited until this morning to complain? Don't you find that the least bit odd? Does he have a picture of the hair?"

"Yes, I do find it odd, but apparently he's a busy man. I don't believe that he has photos of the hairs," the Chef shrugged.

"Who is this busy man?" Susannah growled.

"Ironically enough, he's the town veterinarian," Andre sighed, as Susannah's blood ran cold.

"Bradley Dobbins?" she whispered, eyes narrowed.

"The very same."

"He's made me go out to the dining room twice recently so that he could thank me, and now he's complaining about animal hair in the food? How does he know that the hair didn't fall off of him and into the food?"

"I have no idea. All I know is that we have a formerly happy customer, who is now an unhappy customer."

"Wait a minute…there's a reason for this. What does he want?"

"An apology. The very next time that he comes in. And he wants you to cook him a "decent" meal."

Susannah's blood boiled. The vet had hit her where it hurts. Say what you will about her life, her appearance, any number of things, and she could shrug it off without a second thought, but criticize about her cooking and you might just end up missing a limb or two…if you're lucky.

"How does he presume to know that I'm the one who cooked the meal?" she asked through her teeth.

"He asked."

"So he had enough time to ask who cooked it, but not enough time to make a complaint?"

"Some people prefer not to be confrontational. They would rather call in later than address it when they're upset."

"What if I don't apologize?" Susannah bit her cheek to try to keep a lid on her temper.

"I would not advise that," Andre sighed.

"What if I don't apologize?" she repeated, shaking with anger.

"You'll most likely be fired."

"Fired?"

"Fired," he nodded. "This is a relatively small community, and he's already made noises about going public with the story if you don't make it up to him."

"Bastard," Susannah fumed.

"Agreed. However, he is a high profile bastard, so there is some ass-kissing required here," Andre looked at her pointedly.

"I don't ass-kiss," she muttered.

"You can either kiss ass once and go about your business here, or you can refuse, and try to find another

Assistant Chef position in this town," Andre replied, ever the realist. "I hate this as much as you do, Susannah, but it is the reality of being in a consumer-driven industry. An apology is in order, and you will apologize. Are we in agreement?" he raised an eyebrow.

"Fine."

"Good. I'll call the irritating gentleman personally and ask him when he'd like to come in. I want you to be pleasant and professional in dealing with him."

"Of course," Susannah agreed, a strange look on her face.

Andre stared at her for a long moment.

"Your contribution to this establishment is highly valued, Susannah, I hope you know that," he said quietly.

"Thanks," she tried to smile and failed, miserably.

"I'll let you know when he'll be coming in."

"Can't wait," she rolled her eyes and rose from her chair. "We done?"

"We are indeed," he replied, watching her go.

CHAPTER 32

Bradley Dobbins straightened his tie and sipped at a lovely Pinot Noir which, tonight, was free. He was determined to milk the status he'd achieved by registering a complaint for as much and as long as he could. He would order every expensive item that took his fancy, and a few days later, he would complain again. He planned to repeat the cycle either until the restaurant denied him entry, or until Susannah was fired, which was what he was hoping.

He'd gotten nowhere when he visited Timothy Eckels at the mortuary, so he figured he'd try to take the back door, the mortician's wife, as a means of getting him. The plan was to make Tim angry enough that he'd get careless, and Bradley would be there to reveal him as a serial killer. He knew in his bones that the mortician was hiding something, and he firmly believed that Sheriff Arlen Bemis had arrested the wrong man.

When Susannah Eckels approached his table, she seemed to be glowing with an odd kind of excitement, which he found strangely disturbing. Perhaps she had a bit of a crush on him, and was actually enjoying the extra attention. If threats and trying to get her fired didn't work, he could always flirt with her, lead her on, and encourage her to reveal whatever she might know about her husband's activities. Bradley Dobbins knew he was a handsome man, and if she had elected to marry the bloated cadaver who was Timothy Eckels, she'd be positively swept off her feet by a handsome, successful catch like himself. He'd never touch her of course, but he'd employ a proven system of reeling her in, then holding her at arm's length, in order to underscore her attraction to him.

"Good evening Mrs. Eckels," he greeted her, making certain that she took notice of his devastating dimples.

"Good evening Mr. Dobbins," she replied tonelessly.

"Dr. Dobbins," he corrected.

"Yes of course. Dr. Dobbins. I apologize that you weren't satisfied with your food when you dined here last week," her voice was wooden, a frozen smile pasted on her face.

"You wouldn't have been satisfied either, Susannah," he used his most seductive voice and look.

"I'm not satisfied with anything less than perfection when it comes to my food, Dr. Dobbins," she replied, holding his gaze.

"Obviously you're a woman who can appreciate… good food," his gaze traveled up and down her body, then he switched tactics. "Which is why I found it particularly disappointing that you allowed such filth to come from your kitchen."

Susannah showed no outward reaction, he couldn't gauge whether or not he was getting to her.

"I'm terribly sorry," her voice and face remained blank, neutral. "What would you like to try for this evening's meal?"

"Something without animal hair in it for one thing," he quirked an eyebrow at her.

"Hold the hair, got it. Anything else?"

Brad leaned forward, putting his head on his hand and gazing at her with a boyish smile.

"You hate it, don't you Susannah? It bothers you when someone criticizes your cooking, doesn't it? Gets under your skin…" he chuckled warmly, again getting no reaction from Susannah.

She stared at him.

"I'm not sure that I know what you're talking about, but I assure you that I'll create a fabulous dish for you this evening."

"Hmm…a tough cookie, eh? Okay," he nodded with a smirk, and proceeded to order three appetizers, the daily special, soup, salad, and two desserts. "And make it snappy, I have other engagements," he demanded with a pleasant smile.

Susannah's blood boiled, but outwardly, she remained as cool as a cucumber. Fortunately, the veterinarian had come in at a time when they'd normally be busy, but tonight the crowd was light.

"Tanner, I need your help," she barked, coming into the kitchen.

"Sure thing," the young man replied, putting down a large box of potatoes.

"Does your phone have the ability to record video?"

"Of course, why?"

"You're going to track my every move for the next half an hour, can you record that much?"

"Yeah, but why? Are you making a cooking show?" Tanner was confused.

"No. Instead of kissing ass, I'm going to be covering it," Susannah replied with a strange smile on her face.

"Umm…okay," the young man replied, pulling his phone out of his pocket. "What specifically do you want me to record?"

"The food. Keep your camera on the food at all times."

"Got it. Okay, are you ready?"

"Let's do this," she nodded grimly, and he turned the recording feature on, following Susannah as she went about making the vet's food from start to finish, including after it went to garnishing, and when the servers picked it up to bring to the table.

Bradley Dobbins called for Susannah to come to the table when each item was served, and had her stand there while he tasted it, which Tanner discreetly recorded from the corner of the room. After he'd had his last taste of dessert, he asked for her yet again. When she stood obediently by the table for the last time of the evening, he leaned back in his chair contentedly, locking his fingers behind his head and sucking imaginary particles out of his teeth.

"Well, Miss Susannah, that was a mighty fine spread you prepared," he nodded his approval.

"Thank you," she replied formally.

"Don't even begin to think that this is over," he smiled smugly. "I'm going to continue to be a thorn in your side until your husband admits to what he's doing. How do you feel about that Susannah?" Dobbins asked as pleasantly as if he were inquiring about the weather.

"I'm glad that you enjoyed your dinner. Have a nice

evening." Susannah turned to go and Dobbins tried to grab her, as he'd done before.

Anticipating his intentions, Susannah dodged gracefully out of reach, nearly sending the veterinarian sprawling.

"I'll be back Susannah," he chuckled nastily.

Susannah's insides churned as though she was inhabited by a writhing ball of angrily squirming snakes. She'd gone along, she'd apologized, she'd played nice, all the while wanting to tear Bradley Dobbins from his chair and set upon him with sharp instruments. He'd enjoyed tormenting her, thriving on her discomfort, but she hadn't given an inch. He'd never see her sweat, no matter what sorts of internal resources she had to draw from to stay strong. She would bide her time, and then she would strike, and when she did, the smug Dr. Bradley Dobbins would wish that he'd never been born.

Knowing that men like him were never even remotely interested in women like her, Susannah found it repulsive when he'd turned on the flirtatious charm. She'd make him pay for his nonchalant familiarity, she'd make him pay hard. Her father had made it quite clear her entire life that she was plain, fat, and completely undesirable. She knew her limitations and accepted them. For this arrogant bastard to taunt her by acting as though she might be a fun plaything, was offensive to the extreme, and Susannah didn't take offense lightly.

She wanted to kill him, wanted to take her time in killing him, making him stare at her while he suffered. She'd arrange to have him wide awake and aware while she did a myriad of unspeakable things to him. The knowledge that he was going to die would be an obvious and tangible thing to him. He'd know it, see it, hear it, smell it…taste it. Normally a "clean" killer, Susannah had visions of bathing in Bradley Dobbins blood, swimming in it, reveling in it. If the vet had any idea of what was flashing through her mind while he attempted to verbally torment her, he'd have run screaming into the night, never looking back.

Oh yes, Susannah had a special endgame planned for Bradley, and in the meantime, she wanted to keep him as paranoid and scared as possible. She hated that he'd chosen to direct his anger at her innocent

Timmy, but sometimes innocents got caught in the crossfire. Considering the matter carefully, she felt that Timothy would probably prefer to have her interact with the vet, rather than having to deal with him directly. She was much more equipped to handle difficult people in a manner which seemed socially acceptable...oh the screaming irony.

Meanwhile, the urge to take the life of the vet burned within her, consuming her thoughts, causing her hands to shake. For the first time in a very long while, she felt as though she might have to take another life in order to quiet the rising darkness within. She hated to do it, but she found herself looking at those around her to see who might be abusing their power, and why. If she happened to discover a tyrant who took advantage of others, she might be able to do the world a favor and let their lifeblood ebb from them, ending their tyrannical reign and feeding her need. It was akin to public service, really.

CHAPTER 33

Tanner was more than grateful that he'd trained Elmo to stay quiet whenever someone came to the door. He'd been working on a rabbit that he'd discovered run down on the road, when a knock unexpectedly sounded at his door. Heart thumping, he stood over his latest project, which was splayed out over his tiny kitchen table, wondering what he should do. He stayed motionless, hoping that whoever it was would just go away, but pressed his lips together in frustration when the knock sounded again, more loudly this time.

"Hang on," he called out, hurriedly throwing the tools of his hobby onto the large flattened cardboard box that he was using on top of the table as a work surface.

He picked up the cardboard, and balancing it carefully so that nothing would tip off of it, he walked quickly to his bedroom, lying the project on the floor in front of his closet. The apartment was small, so there was nowhere else to stash it where it wouldn't be seen by his drop-in visitor. Elmo followed him, sniffing at the rabbit curiously, his brilliant red plume of a tail swishing back and forth.

"Stay here. Good boy," Tanner whispered, scratching Elmo's head between his ears and closing the bedroom door.

As he walked back toward the bedroom, the knocking sounded again, even more insistent this time. The young man opened it, shocked to see his boss on the stoop.

"Doc?" he frowned, wondering what on earth the veterinarian was doing in this part of town.

"Evening Tanner," the smile didn't quite reach his eyes. "May I come in?"

"Umm…okay. My place is like…small and gross, but…" the young man shrugged.

"I'm sure it's fine, this won't take long," the vet insisted, awakening suspicion in his employee.

Tanner opened the door wider, letting his boss in, and gestured to the shabby couch that was the only piece of furniture in his miniscule living room. Grabbing a chair from the kitchen table, he sat down facing Bradley Dobbins, feeling very strange.

"So, what's up?" he asked, his face impassive.

"I have a proposition for you, young man," an unholy light seemed to gleam in the veterinarian's eyes. "How would you like to make a great deal of money?"

"I've always wanted to go to college..." Tanner replied carefully.

"I need you to do something for me, and I'll send you to college and then some," Dobbins smirked.

"I'm listening."

Timothy Eckels had a dilemma of major proportions. He had a fresh body on the slab that needed to be prepared for a memorial service the following day, and an emergency pickup order had just come in from the sheriff, who insisted that he come out right away. If he did the irascible sheriff's bidding, he wouldn't have nearly enough time to go through the embalming and preparation procedures that needed to occur in order to have the body on his metal table ready to meet his friends and loved ones for the last time tomorrow. Tanner came bounding down the stairs and saw that his boss was visibly distressed.

"What's wrong?" the perceptive young man asked.

"There aren't enough hours in the day," Tim muttered, torn between the task at hand, and the absolute reality of incurring the sheriff's wrath if he didn't show for the pickup. The less than bright lawman already thought that Tim might be capable of murder, and was looking for any reason to hassle him.

"Do you need some help? What can I do?" Tanner asked.

"Well, the sheriff will never turn over a body to you, and you wouldn't know how to transport it anyway," the mortician sighed. "And you can't exactly start the embalming process for me, so, no, I don't think you can help."

"I can do the exsanguination and preservation for you. I've seen you do it lots of times. After I'm done, I can finish the cavity prep and get him dressed, so that all you have to do tomorrow is put on the finishing touches," Tanner suggested.

"You haven't been properly educated," Tim frowned, inwardly admitting that the idea had appeal.

"You've seen my taxidermy. It's pretty much the same process, and I'm very precise."

"I suppose you could always call me with any questions," the mortician pursed his lips. "And I'd most likely be back here with the next body before you even got to the cavity prep."

"Then go," Tanner suggested. "I've got this."

"I could lose my license if anyone ever found out about this. No, I don't think it's a good idea," Tim shook his head firmly. The phone on the wall in the prep room jangled loudly, startling both of them.

"Hello?" Tim answered, impatient.

Tanner could hear the sheriff's tirade as Tim held the phone away from his ear.

"I understand. Yes, I'll be there shortly," his jaw flexed.

"Should I prepare your equipment?" Tanner asked when his boss hung up the phone.

"Please," Tim nodded. "I'll be back as quickly as I can."

Tim had the address that the sheriff had given him written on a page in his cadaver log. He kept track of every pickup, the dates, times, places and circumstances of each visit, knowing that such details might be important later. He flipped open the current page and verified that the mailbox that he was in front of indeed marked the driveway of the deceased. He'd driven to the middle of nowhere, and there was no house in sight, just a lane that led into a stand of trees, and a battered and rusted mailbox.

"Yes, 4312 Warner Rd., this is it," he muttered to himself.

He pulled into the lane and drove slowly on the barely-there path through the woods, finally rounding a bend a couple miles in, and caught sight of the sheriff's car. He pulled up and noted that Arlen Bemis was standing on the front porch of a shabby house that had pile after pile of random items stacked at least six feet high all across the porch. The sheriff looked decidedly sour, and Tim found himself hoping that the surly man wouldn't be abusive.

"Bout time, Eckels," Bemis growled as Tim climbed the rickety steps to the porch. "Thought you'd decided to friggin' walk out here or something. Stiff's in the back bedroom. Now that you're here, I can finally get home and attend to my dinner. Next of kin is in the living room. Have fun," Arlen smirked, heading toward his car.

"Shouldn't you stay until I get him out?" Tim called after him.

"Nope, he's all yours now, not my problem," the sheriff plunked down into the driver's seat and shut the car door before Tim could respond.

The introverted mortician felt decidedly awkward having to open the front door of the shack and enter by himself, but the sooner that he got in there, the sooner he'd be able to get back to his work at the mortuary. He had a funeral to prepare for. Taking a breath, determined to be brave, Timothy opened the door and the first thing that hit him was the smell. There was death, that was certain. He'd smelled that sickly sweet odor more times than he could count, but there was also something more...much more. The cacophony of scent nearly overwhelmed him, stinging his eyes and irritating his throat and the lining of his nostrils. There was a pungent smell of ammonia and animal waste, as though several cats lived in the home and had no litter boxes, and an underlying stench of rot – rotted food, rotted plaster and wood, and rotted teeth.

The door could only be opened about eighteen inches because there were more piles of random stuff, newspapers, cans, bottles, clothing, bags of trash, and a huge assortment of cheap and broken household items, stacked up to the low ceiling of the filthy home. Tim sidled in, thankful that he wasn't a large man, and tried to take shallow breaths, feeling less than safe about the fouled air entering his lungs.

He walked down the only hall that was accessible from the doorway, and saw a scraggly-haired woman sitting in a recliner with stuffing poking out of it, a one-eyed mangy cat in her lap.

"You the funeral guy?" she asked, and when she opened her mouth to speak, he saw now why there was a pervasive rotted tooth smell in the home.

"Uh, yes, that's right," he nodded, hating how it tasted when he breathed through his mouth.

"My baby's in the back," her lower lip trembled and she pointed a shaky finger in the direction that Tim had been heading.

"Thank you. I'm sorry for your loss," he replied, ducking out and wondering what sort of state the deceased must be in if this was the condition of the living in the home.

There were only two doors in the hall, an appalling bathroom on the left, and what may have been a bedroom on the right. The hall and each room, including the bathroom, was stuffed with more refuse. Tim had heard of hoarders before, and had gone into many different homes that had been cluttered, dirty, or both, but had never encountered anything like this in his life. Just before he entered the bedroom to look for the body, another thin-as-a-rail cat skittered out ahead of him.

The smell of death grew stronger, letting him know that somewhere in the dank confines ahead of him, lay a body. One that had been expired for quite some time if his nose served him correctly. Shimmying between stacks of newspapers piled precariously on either side of the door, Tim made his way into the room, scanning to try to find the body, conscious that time was ticking away. He saw a pile in one corner that seemed higher than the others, and, taking a closer look, spotted a foot, ironically clad in a running shoe, sticking out of the mess. If the size of the foot was any indication as to the size of the body, Tim had no idea how he was going to get the man on his gurney and into the hearse. He made a few notes in his notebook, and made his way carefully over to the body, slipping once in what looked like a fresh pile of cat poop, but recovering quickly enough that he didn't fall.

Thankful for his nitrile gloves, the mortician started grabbing plastic bags filled with who-knows-what and tossing them to the other side of the room, revealing a leg that looked like it was thicker around than his somewhat pudgy waist. He stopped for a moment, glanced at the narrow door frame, then back at the leg, and sighed. After nearly half an hour, Tim had most of the morbidly obese man uncovered. How the coroner had made a determination that there was no foul play involved in the man's demise was anyone's guess, but the mortician was more focused on how he was going to transport such a massive body. If he was even able to get the corpse out of the house, which was a task he definitely couldn't accomplish by himself, he didn't know for certain if the deceased would fit in the hearse. He needed to call for help, which would make the operation take that much longer.

By the time that the ambulance had arrived, Tim had cleared all of the debris from the area immediately surrounding the young man who had apparently died of asphyxiation when he had become wedged in the corner of his bedroom, unable to rise from the bed.

"We're not going to be able to get him through that door," the EMT, who wore a surgical mask over his face, shook his head. His partner had caught one whiff of the stench in the house and was presently leaning over the porch rail heaving up his dinner.

"I don't believe we have a choice. I can't prepare him

for burial here," Tim commented, trying not to glance at his watch.

"Seems like he's already buried," the EMT looked around the room in disgust.

"What do we need to do?" Tim demanded, his patience running short.

"Gotta call the fire department. We need an extraction," he shrugged. "I'll go check on my partner and let them know that we need an extraction unit."

"How long will that take?"

"They probably won't even get here for a bit, then they have to set up their equipment and then the actual work happens. Once they gain access in here, there's the matter of using a special crane to get him in the ambulance, then we have to start the whole process all over again when we unload him at your place. We're in this one for the long hall, buddy," the EMT shook his head.

By the time Timothy Eckels got back to the mortuary, and had secured the new corpse in a walk-in cooler, it was nearly three o'clock in the morning, and he was utterly exhausted. He pulled out the drawer containing the body of Myron Biggs, the young man he'd been working on earlier, and was actually relieved to see that Tanner, against his wishes, had finished the prepping of the body, with the exception of the cosmetic work, which would take no time at all. Tim could theoretically sleep in tomorrow and still have enough time to prepare Myron prior to his funeral tomorrow evening. The weary mortician shut off the lights, locked up the mortuary, and was so tired when he finally staggered into bed, that he noticed, but didn't care, that his wife wasn't there.

CHAPTER 34

Tanner seemed a bit too preoccupied as he went about his prep duties at Le Chateau, barely glancing at Susannah, even when she handed him a box of salmon to gut and filet.

"Everything okay?" she asked, wondering if she might just have to kill him after all.

"Yeah, I'm fine. I think I may be coming down with something," he mumbled.

Though she was several feel from him, Susannah instinctively stepped back and made certain that she was breathing through her nose.

"Then you shouldn't be preparing food," she insisted, wanting all possibility of germs out of her kitchen. If she became ill due to exposure to Tanner, she wouldn't have any qualms at all about killing him. "You need to go home."

"Okay," he agreed, still not looking at her. He put down his knife, peeled off his gloves and untied his apron, heading for the door.

"Hope you feel better," Susannah called out, darting to the supply room for disinfectant.

The young man shuffled, head down, the bracing autumn air assaulting him through the worn cloth of his jacket. He hadn't slept last night, and should have been relieved in a way – there would soon be a significant amount of money in his account, thanks to Bradley Dobbins. He felt guilty that he wouldn't be going to the mortuary today, and was sad about the fact that he probably would never be going back again. He'd enjoyed the quiet, steady company of the introverted man who'd used human flesh as his canvas and brought the dead to life for one last goodbye. He felt as though he understood Timothy Eckels, who preferred his solitary world to the one in which the rest of humanity lived and breathed. People could be awful to each other, and it had scarred the sensitive youth more than he cared to admit.

Timothy Eckels was not one who was general moved by emotions, either positive or negative, but something had been niggling at his psyche all day. Something just didn't feel right. He tried to pass it off as lack of sleep from his eventful night, or maybe the fact that his wife hadn't come to bed until nearly six a.m., but the churning low in his gut that put his animal instincts on edge, just wouldn't go away. The mortician didn't have time to focus on his misgivings however, he had a funeral to prepare for, and it was going to be a big one. Local newspaper reporter Myron Biggs had passed away from a heart attack the day before, and the turnout for his memorial service tonight promised to be standing-room only. Why Myron's next of kin had demanded such a quick turn-around time was a mystery, but thanks to some less-than-official help from Tanner, Tim would be able to accommodate them.

The sliding panels between mourning rooms had all been opened in anticipation of overflow crowds, with the casket to be placed in the middle room. There would be three hours designated for the final viewing, with a memorial service to follow. Thankfully, the wake would be held at the country club, so at least Tim wouldn't have to stay up late two nights in a row. Susannah was working tonight, so he'd be on his own for dinner after the funeral, and quite frankly, he was looking forward to the down time.

Preparing Myron for his viewing had been a breeze after Tanner had done nearly everything the night before, while Tim had been mired down in the extrication of an overly large corpse. A quick application of makeup on the somehow still-supple skin of the reporter had been all it took to make him presentable and lifelike. Tim admired the skill and eye for detail that his young protégé had exhibited, and thought that Tanner would make a capable assistant mortician. He might even be willing to foot the bill so that he could go to mortuary school. He'd been disappointed when the young man hadn't shown up to work today, but would tell him of his thoughts when he saw him next. The mortician glanced at his watch and his stomach turned over with the realization that crowds of mourners would begin showing up in roughly half an hour. That gave him time to change into his oh-so-sober suit and tie, and take a breath to prepare for dealing with the public, his least favorite task.

The viewing had proceeded according to plan, and the mourners filed into the largest center room for the memorial service. Tim was more than glad to hand the reigns of the service off to Pastor Waylan Fartham, who shepherded the flock over at the Methodist church, where Myron and his family were members. The tough part was over. Now all he had to do was stand respectfully in the corner of the room behind the Pastor until the service concluded, then transport the body and set up the casket at the cemetery, and he could call it a day.

"Friends and loved ones," the Pastor's usually big booming voice was subdued a bit. "Let us begin today with a moment of silent prayer, where we reflect upon the precious fragility of life, and our never-ending bond with our Creator and each other. Please bow your heads."

Silence, glorious silence. Tim was often offended when soft coughs, rustling or restlessness interrupted the silence. It held no holiness for him, but the absence of human interaction and opinion helped him to relax. This time however, the sound that he heard didn't offend him, it sent a bolt of sheer terror surging through his body. He literally, physically jumped, his head snapping up so hard that his neck cracked.

Thump, thump, thump. Mmmmmmm!

A haunting reality that the mortician had heretofore only experienced in his most heart-stopping night-mares had just occurred right in front of him. The noise was coming from Myron's casket. There was a collective gasp and more than a few screams as Tim rushed to the casket, only to be shouldered out of the way by Sheriff Arlen Bemis, who lifted the lid to reveal a wide-eyed and clearly hysterical Myron Biggs, whose lips were sewn securely shut, muffling his screams.

The sheriff had dismissed Tim, telling him to go home while the Biggs family decided whether or not they were going to press charges. At the very least, his mortician's credentials would be revoked, and he'd be out of business. This was what he got for giving someone a chance, this was what he got for trusting Tanner to do the job that only he should've done. His career, his life, his reason for being had just been flushed down the tubes in one fell swoop. He had done the unthinkable. He had almost buried a living human being. But how? He'd had no indication that Myron Biggs was alive. There was no movement and no pulse, but he *had* noticed the odd pliability of Myron's skin, which should have tipped him off.

His wife wasn't home when he arrived, and he was glad, preferring to grieve alone. He thought about his enigmatic mate, found his thoughts wandering toward the solace that she received from her hobbies and suddenly found himself compelled to explore her solitary realm again. Maybe he would see the peace and beauty in her art that she saw. Maybe he could somehow draw strength and hope from seeing his wife's creations. At the very least, it would feel better than sitting hopelessly in his darkened living room, lost and ashamed.

Donning a well-worn cardigan to ward off the basement's chill, Tim headed down the stairs hoping to at least take his mind off of his current situation. He reached the door at the bottom of the stairs and was surprised to find that it had been padlocked. When had that happened? He didn't have long to puzzle over the sudden appearance of the lock, because his doorbell rang urgently, three times in a row. He seriously contemplated just hiding out in the basement stairwell until his caller went away, but when a fierce knocking began, he realized that whoever was on the other side of the front door, wasn't giving up easily. Sighing, Tim trudged up the stairs, in no particular hurry, and shuffled to the door, where the persistent person on the other side was still knocking.

"Mr. Eckels, I know you probably don't want to see me right now, but I have to tell you something important," Tanner put his hand on the door to prevent the mortician from slamming it in his face.

Timothy stared at the young man in disbelief, blinking at him from behind his thick glasses.

"I can't think of anything that I'd want to hear from you right now," he replied, stone-faced.

"But you have to, because..." his sentence was cut short by flashing lights and the whoop of a siren as two police cars rounded the corner.

Tanner's eyes went wide and he let out a startled exclamation, diving for the bushes which shielded the side of the porch from street view. In seconds, he'd disappeared, and Tim stood in the doorway as the sheriff and a host of deputies pulled into the drive beside his house.

CHAPTER 35

Susannah Eckels had lied to her husband. She wasn't scheduled to work this evening, she'd called off, telling Andre that she needed to help Tim out with Myron Biggs's funeral, so while her boss thought she was with Tim, and Tim thought that she was at work, she had actually been preparing to pull off her most creative bloodletting yet. She'd plotted for months to torture Bradley Dobbins as much as possible before she finally killed him, and she planned to get very inventive in harvesting souvenirs from the arrogant bastard as well. He'd wish that he had never attempted to flirt with or otherwise offend Susannah Eckels. She wouldn't let him scream either. He'd have to suffer in silence, and it would be glorious, her crowning achievement. The sins of all controlling, manipulative mankind would be paid by this despicable sacrificial lamb.

She had gotten to his house early, just after dusk, slipping into the neighborhood through the woods, and keeping to alleys and side yards so she wouldn't be spotted. Even after she'd taunted him, Bradley Dobbins had been too stubborn and cheap to put in an actual alarm system, so she let herself in easily, and hid in his closet, slipping on a pair of his sandals and waiting for him to come home to meet his doom. She had only one object in her pocket, a chloroform-saturated handkerchief, secured in a plastic bag. Once she had effectively used that, she'd choose her instruments of torture from among the veterinarian's extensive collection of sharp, blunt, and potentially lethal or painful items. There were kitchen knives, yard tools, and just plain ordinary household items galore that would serve as wonderfully effective implements of bodily harm, she was giddy just thinking about it. Tim had better be ready for action when she got home, her senses were heightened and her libido was rising, and Brad's blood hadn't even started flowing yet.

Susannah shivered with delight when she heard the purr of his car engine pulling into the attached garage.

She had already scoped out the locations of the duct tape that she would use to secure him, the socks with which she'd keep him quiet, and the best surface on which to do her handiwork. Now, it was only a matter of time.

Bradley Dobbins whistled a cheery tune. His plan to run Timothy Eckels and his strangely unappealing wife out of town had gone off without a hitch. It had cost him, dearly, but it was worth every penny. The kid had done what he was supposed to do, and Dobbins would refuse to give him a dime of the money that he had promised. What was the kid going to do? Call the cops? Nope, the investment that had been made was in buying the cooperation of Myron Biggs, which had taken some tall talking and lots of zeros. Myron had owed Bradley a favor, after the veterinarian had stumbled upon the reporter with his pants down…quite literally, while in the company of a male prostitute. The vet didn't look upon his proposition as blackmail, but more like two businessmen ensuring each other's success. He smirked when he thought of the abject terror he'd seen in Myron's eyes when he'd been busted doing unspeakable things to a thin, tattooed young man in a public park. Price you pay for not being careful.

Now, after a hard day's work, Bradley was going to take a long hot shower, order a pizza and stuff himself silly while watching TV with a six pack of craft beer. Assured that his business would be safe from a crusading pet lover, he could start daydreaming about his Caribbean retirement again. It had taken some creativity, but finally, Dobbins' life was back on track, without any pesky interference from animal lovers.

Entirely unaware of the woman crouching behind the garment bags in the corner of his closet, Brad stripped down, tossing his clothes into the hamper of the walk-in, and padded off to the shower. Susannah nearly gasped in her need to possess his life force, to hold it in her hands and toy with it, but she stayed silent as a ghost until she heard the water running and the shower door click shut behind him.

Slinking out into the living room, where she'd observed him often enough to know his routine, she slipped into the space between the back of the couch and the wall, directly behind where he always sat, waiting to make her move.

While Brad was showering, the hair on the back of his neck raised, inexplicably, and he stood still for a moment, trying to listen over the sound of the running water. Hearing nothing and convincing himself that he was just jumping at shadows, he finished lathering up and rinsing before turning the water off and stepping out into the steamy confines of his spotless bathroom. He toweled dry, and ran his hands through his hair to straighten it, before heading back to his bedroom. He planned to dress in comfortable athletic clothes before his pizza was delivered, but, feeling saucy, he strutted out to the living room completely naked, a soft erection forming at his crotch. He hoped that the person who answered the phone at Papa Guido's was female, and he thought about satisfying one of his hungers before the pizza arrived.

Peeking around the corner of the couch, Susannah saw Brad's semi-tumescent state and nearly giggled, catching herself in the nick of time. He was certainly feeling his oats today…which would make her triumph that much sweeter. Hoping that he'd sit in his favorite spot before making the phone call to the pizza place, she grinned from ear to ear when she heard the couch springs creak under his weight. He tapped out the number, and when she heard the ringing on the other end, she knew she had to strike. If he had time to place his order, she'd have to kill the delivery guy too, and that wasn't part of the plan.

"Papa Guido's," a cheery, feminine voice announced on the other end of the phone.

Before Brad could answer, Susannah popped up behind the couch, secured the veterinarian in a head-lock, disgusted to see that he'd had one hand on the phone and the other in his lap, and pressed the chloro-formed cloth to his nose and mouth. He dropped the phone, trying to break free of his attacker's iron grip, and struggled mightily, but due to the angle of her hold and the element of surprise, he was ineffective in his efforts, and eventually succumbed.

"Hello? Anybody there?" the young woman who had answered the call asked, before cursing and hanging up.

Susannah's eyes traveled greedily up and down the limp body which was now sprawled on the couch, fixating on the pulse throbbing in his neck.

"Oh Doggie Doctor, we're gonna have some fun," she chuckled, then ran to the kitchen for the duct tape.

Bradley Dobbins had one hell of a headache. He tried to move and couldn't. His eyes shot open, darting about in anger and terror, and the first thing that swam into his vision was the bland face of Susannah Eckels. Infuriated, he tried desperately to move, but found that, as he lay on his back in the middle of the kitchen floor, his hands were secured at the wrists and somehow fastened to the floor, his legs were bound together at the ankles and knees and secured to the floor, and duct tape criss-crossed his torso, head and neck securing him to the floor. He was covered in the strong, sticky stuff, and a strip had been placed across his mouth for good measure.

He tried to scream at the woman hovering above him with a psychotic smile, but his efforts only resulted in a high pitched, muffled sound coming out of his nose. He kept it up until Susannah, tiring of the noise, leaned over and pinched his nostrils shut. His faced reddened, then purpled from lack of air, and just as he was on the verge of passing out, she released her hold, letting him choke down precious breaths, his eyes watering.

"Naughty boy," Susannah admonished. "It won't go

well for you if you try to make noise. How does it feel?" she asked.

Bradley's brow furrowed.

"Oh, is that a confusing question? Let me be more clear...how does it feel being completely helpless? Knowing that the power of life and death is in my capable hands...how does that feel?" she smiled in a predatory manner that seemed to agitate the doctor.

"That's what I wanted to see," she practically purred, feeling the tension and fear emanating from the naked and vulnerable man.

Susannah picked up a butcher knife that she had lying on a towel next to where she knelt beside Bradley's head, along with some other particularly interesting painmakers, and held it up, admiring the glimmer of light along the blade.

"You really should sharpen your knives you know," she mused, dangling the knife inches from his nose as his eyes went wide with fear. "See, when they're not sharp, they tend to tear the flesh, rather than slicing through it nice and easy, and that's just a shame. Sloppy really," she remarked, being entirely honest. "Here, let me show you."

Dobbins' chest heaved as he panted quick, scared breaths through his nose, his eyes on the blade that she lowered next to his cheek.

"You have enormous ears," the killer commented. "They'll make perfect flowers for my skin tree," she murmured, bending down to get a closer look.

The veterinarian felt a searing pain shooting through the side of his head and screamed through his nose. Susannah let out an exaggerated sigh.

"I told you not to do that," she said, pinching his nose shut again, this time allowing him to pass out.

The skin artist took advantage of the fact that her source material had gone quiet, and cut off not just one, but both ears, tucking them into a bag that she'd take home when she was done. When Bradley came to this time, he immediately began a low, continuous keening sound through his nose that Susannah found not just tolerable, but somehow actually satisfying.

"Yeah, that's gotta hurt," she commented, nodding. "This will too."

She'd noticed a pattern of moles on the veterinarian's ribs that almost formed the shape of a heart, so she took a pair of hair cutting scissors that she'd found in the bathroom, and began snipping a heart shaped piece of flesh out of Bradley's side, careful to get only the topmost layers of skin. The skin itself was supple, giving way after stretching a bit between the blades of the shears, and she was thankful that he apparently moisturized fairly regularly – it was great for making nice, smooth pieces, even after dehydration. His ears and side bled profusely, and she let them, placing kitchen towels on either side of his head and beside his body, to keep the blood from pooling around him.

"Don't worry. I noticed that you had your Persian carpet cleaned, so I brought you out here. It would be a shame to ruin such a lovely rug," Susannah assured the terrified bleeding man who begged her with his eyes.

"Oh, don't look so sad. I'm just showing you how it feels when someone treats you like they own you. This pain," she jabbed a gloved finger into the raw cut where his left ear used to be and he nearly fainted again. "This pain is nothing compared to having a father who hates you," she explained bitterly.

Bradley Dobbins couldn't control the tears if he wanted to, they flowed over the wounds on the sides of his head, mingling with his blood. He couldn't control other bodily functions either, and Susannah shook her head in disapproval when his bladder voided.

"That's just gross. I intended to be somewhat gentle and to get this done rather quickly, but now I'm going to have to let you suffer."

She nicked an artery in his thigh with medical precision. He'd bleed out eventually, but he had a lot of pain to endure before he did. Once the cut was made, she went about harvesting various body parts and skin pieces for her artwork, pausing periodically to strategically place more towels on the veterinarian as rich, metallic-scented blood oozed from him, becoming more and more sluggish as his heart worked harder and harder to pump less and less. By the time she was done, Bradley Dobbins, who was still very much alive and out of his mind with pain, looked like a patchwork quilt that had been doused in blood.

"Well Doctor, I believe that my work here is done. I normally like to watch the last spark of life slip away from the oppressors, but you disgust me, so I'm not going to dignify you by witnessing your surrender. You're going to die hurting and alone, and I'm going to feel a tremendous amount of satisfaction about that," she explained, slipping off her gloves and stashing them in the bag with various parts of Bradley that she'd harvested.

Susannah stood to go, placing her hands in the small of her back, stretching to get the kinks out, after having knelt so long, and was suddenly blinded by a piercing light which shone through the sliding doors in the kitchen.

"Put your hands behind your head and freeze!" Sheriff Arlen Bemis ordered from the other side of the glass, as a deputy came crashing through the front door.

Knowing that there was no escape, Susannah smiled a secret smile and did as she was told.

Law enforcement came charging into Bradley Dobbins' home from all directions, horrified at carnage on display, and two deputies began working frantically at the duct tape, while a third was tasked with handcuffing and escorting Susannah to his patrol car.

"Oh..." Susannah paled and slumped like she was going to faint.

The deputy reflexively moved to slide his hands down beneath her armpits to keep her from falling to the floor, which turned out to be a grave mistake on his part. Susannah snapped out of her ruse and elbowed the deputy in the crotch, hard. When he fell to his knees, she scrambled out the door, brushing past a startled and somewhat out of shape Sheriff Bemis, who immediately wheeled around and ran after the fleeing fugitive.

"Backup!" he huffed over his shoulder, trying desperately to keep up with the woman who was now more than familiar with the dark alleys and side yards of the veterinarian's neighborhood.

Two deputies realized what was happening and came charging past the aging sheriff as Susannah neared the woods. Adrenalin flowed through her like a live wire and she knew that if she could make it to the cover of the trees, she was home free. She had even stashed a bag in the next county, just in case a situation like this ever arose. Her thighs burned, and her lungs wheezed, but she was exhilarated as she heard the footsteps pounding behind her. Twenty more feet and she'd lose them in the trees. Ten. Five. Success.

She darted in and out of the trees, making certain to take a route where there were plenty of tripping hazards of which she was aware and the deputies were not, smiling to herself when she heard the occasional thud or exclamation of pain behind her. As the sounds grew more distant, she knew that she'd be able to relax soon. It would be a bit of time before they had a chance to either get dogs in the woods, or a helicopter in the air, and by then she'd be somewhere in the next county, where the tiny towns were few and far between. She'd planned meticulously for a day just like this one, and it tickled her to realize that she was about to get away with murder, when she'd been right under the sheriff's nose.

Sheriff Arlen Bemis was livid. He'd marshalled every available deputy and officer within several miles of Pellman to join in the chase. He would find Susannah Eckels, and when he did, he'd make sure that she went away for a very long time, permanently if he could swing it. She hadn't gone home, her milquetoast husband had been entirely unaware of his wife's morbid hobby.

"Sheriff, take line one," a deputy popped his head into Arlen's office. "They picked up your fugitive over in Cassel County, they're taking her in right now."

Bemis snatched up his office phone and punched the flashing button. "Don't let her out of your sight, and take every precaution. She'll do whatever unspeakable things that she can think of to get away," he barked into the phone, not bothering with formalities.

After being reassured by the deputy on the line that she'd be secured in the Cassel County jail in no time, Arlen grabbed his keys and ran for the door, knowing that he wouldn't feel secure until Susannah Eckels was in his custody.

CHAPTER 36

Sheriff Arlen Bemis glared at the nervous young man who sat across the desk from him. Tanner Benson had come in of his own accord, saying that he had some information about Timothy and Susannah Eckels.

"If you got something to say, you better start talking, boy. Otherwise you're just wasting my time and I don't take kindly to people who waste my time," Bemis growled.

It had been one helluva night. Bradley Dobbins was in intensive care, and the serial killer that he thought he'd already found, turned out to be Susannah Eckels. The sheriff had to swallow his embarrassment and let the homeless man who'd been named as the murderer out of jail. When he'd seen Bradley's shoes on the woman's feet, he'd figured out what she'd done immediately. She'd worn Jorge's shoes when she killed him, and the homeless guy's shoes when she'd killed the cheerleader. In all his days in law enforcement, Arlen had never encountered as sick a mind as the one behind Susannah Eckels' cold eyes.

"Uh...I just wanted you to know that Mr. Eckels wasn't responsible for the guy who was alive in the coffin."

"Yes, he was responsible. He didn't do his job, and I don't see why that's any of your concern," Bemis replied dismissively.

"He didn't do it. He was set up," Tanner insisted.

"Set up?" The youth had managed to capture the sheriff's attention, and he leaned forward. "What are you talkin' about, boy?"

"I worked for the vet, Dr. Dobbins, and he hated Mr. Eckels for some reason. So he paid me to go get a job at the mortuary, so that I could tell him if Mr. Eckels did anything weird."

This was clearly news to the sheriff, who raised an eyebrow.

"Did he?" Bemis asked.

"Did he what?" Tanner was confused.

"Did Eckels do anything weird?"

The young man shook his head. "No, that's just it. He's like the most by-the-book, boring dude ever, even if he has a cool job."

The sheriff stared at Tanner as he considered that last remark, but moved on.

"So what did Dobbins get out of hiring you to spy on Eckels then?"

"Well, when Mr. Eckels didn't do anything, Dr. Dobbins told me that he'd pay me a bunch of money if I did something for him. He said he'd pay for me to go to school."

"What did he want you to do?"

"He wanted me to pretend to embalm someone who wasn't dead," Tanner confessed, his cheeks coloring with shame. He was still kicking himself for having sold out Tim, who loved animals and had never even made a snide remark about anyone.

"That don't make a lick of sense," Arlen pursed his lips and glared at the young man in front of him.

"But it's true. Doc made a lot of money by treating animals with these stupid supplements that don't work, and he was losing business because people were going to Mr. Eckels to have their pets put to sleep."

"So the fool was right about that," Bemis mused.

"Yeah, but Mr. Eckels stopped doing it, because he couldn't stand taking lives, even animal ones, even when they were suffering."

"He sure as heck picked the wrong mate," the sheriff commented sardonically. "So how in the world did you pretend to embalm someone?" his eyes narrowed in suspicion.

"Doc gave one of his friends some kind of drug that made it look like he was dead, but he really wasn't, and then the guy's family said that the funeral had to be right away so that the drug wouldn't wear off until he was in the coffin."

"That was a stupid risk. What if he hadn't woken up in time?"

"Well, I guess the Doc had practiced with the drug on some of the bigger animals to see how long it took to wear off," Tanner shrugged. "He used pigs I think, and big dogs."

"But why wouldn't Eckels have done the embalming? You're not certified," the sheriff demanded.

"Because that was the night that they had to dig the really big dude out of his house, and Mr. Eckels didn't have time to do it, so I told him that I did. I already had the guy dressed and everything before he came back, so all he had to do was put on some makeup."

"Interesting how those two deaths coincided," Bemis said, more to himself than the young man in front of him. "And why on earth would Myron Biggs, a local celebrity, have gone along with such a scheme?"

"Probably because of these, Sheriff," Tanner pulled a manila envelope out from under his thin jacket. "I found the originals in Doc's office a couple of weeks ago, and I made these copies in case he decided that he didn't want to pay me after I helped him."

Arlen Bemis's face registered shock as he flipped through the photos which showed Myron Biggs in an intimate situation with a young tattooed man, who was bent over a picnic table.

"So, you see, it really wasn't Mr. Eckels fault. Do you think you could maybe talk to that family so that they don't press charges? It was a setup, Sheriff, it wouldn't be right to make him take the fall for all this," Tanner pointed out.

"I'm gonna send a deputy in here and you're going to make an official statement, you understand boy?" Arlen stood and put on his hat.

"Yes sir," Tanner nodded.

"Sit tight, I got some folks to talk to," the sheriff muttered on his way out.

Arlen Bemis was not looking forward to visiting the shack from which David Thurston, the obese young man who had died in bed, had been extricated, but he needed to speak with Verna, the boy's mother. When he pulled up in front of the shack, after his long drive through the country, the sheriff was surprised to see a shiny compact sitting in front of the house. Verna Thurston was loading the little car with a suitcase and what looked like a box of photo albums.

"Afternoon, Ms. Thurston," he greeted the grieving mother, taking off his hat.

"Afternoon, Sheriff," she nodded and set the box of photo albums on the ground beside the car.

"Mind if I talk with you for a minute?" he asked casually, noting that the back seat of the car was already full.

"I ain't got but a few minutes. I'm heading to my sister's soon as I get my stuff loaded," Verna replied, hands on hips.

"Tell you what, you can keep loading up, and I'll help you carry your things while we talk," he offered, glad that he wouldn't have to go inside and stay there.

"That'll work. Mighty kind of ya," she nodded, moving back toward the shack, with Arlen trailing after her.

"You have any visitors last week?"

"Nope, it was just me and David here," Verna called over her shoulder, weaving her way through stacks of trash and grabbing a box of plastic kitchen ware that she handed to the sheriff.

"No one stopped by?" Arlen moved quickly toward the door, trying to take as few breaths as possible.

"Well, now that you mentioned it, the vet came out for a house call right before David passed. My little Ringo had a swollen paw that he took a look at."

"Is he okay?"

"Yeah, he done took off and I ain't seen him since," Verna shrugged.

The sheriff breathed deeply once outside.

"Did the vet visit with David at all?"

"Sure did. Went back and saw him for a bit. He was the last one to see him alive," she started to choke up and Bemis sighed inwardly.

"Looks like you've got a new car," the sheriff commented casually.

"New to me. It's kind of an old car though," she shrugged, avoiding his eyes.

"Where'd you buy it?"

"I didn't."

"Then how did you get it," Arlen persisted.

"Can't say," Verna stared at the ground, kicking at a clump of grass with her worn sneaker.

"Verna, did Doctor Dobbins give you this car?" he prodded.

"He told me not to tell. Said it would mess up his taxes or something. He just felt sorry for me, and I think he was a little sweet on me too," the woman crumbled like a dry cookie. "I don't wanna get him in trouble."

"I understand," Arlen was noncommittal. "Did David typically sleep in the corner of his bed, where the walls meet?"

"No, he usually slept sitting up, under the window. It kept him cooler that way, why?"

"No reason. Listen, I know you've got things to do, so I won't keep you, but can I get your sister's address and phone number before you go?"

CHAPTER 37

Timothy Eckels had been cleared of all possible
charges, and under the circumstances, Sheriff Arlen
Bemis had told him that he wouldn't even be reported
to the Association of Licensed Morticians, so he'd be
able to keep his license. His wife had been
temporarily jailed in the next county while she
awaited her first hearings, because the Pellman jail
was full, and Bradley Dobbins would be going to jail
once he recovered from his injuries.

The veterinary clinic had been shut down, and Tanner
had been promoted to Susannah's position at Le
Chateau. Tim had prepared the remains of David
Thurston for burial, and had locked the doors of the
mortuary forever, giving the keys to a local realtor
with instructions to sell it and wire the money to an

account at a national bank, that he could access from anywhere. Police had emptied the contents of Susannah's basement workshop, finding parts and pieces of human remains which tied her to more murders than most law enforcement professionals see in a lifetime, and the FBI was called in to help track down the multitudes of victims.

Tim packed exactly one suitcase and placed it in the back of his car with regret. He could have made a good life here. He'd had an impeccable reputation, and his work had been satisfying, but now, knowing what his wife had done, he'd been subject to horrified and judgmental stares from strangers and acquaintances everywhere he went. It was only a matter of time before his business dried up and folks ran him out of town anyway, so he'd leave before they had the chance. He never wanted to see Susannah again. He'd been horrified when details about her sick life had been revealed, and people in the grocery store wondered aloud how he could have been married to her for so long and never realized that she was a monster. He wondered the same thing.

Timothy Eckels would never be the same. He thought that he'd never love another human being after his grandmother died, and now he realized that he would've been better off if he'd never tried. That hidden, tender part of his heart was now closed off forever. He'd never trust another human being again.

The mortician had seen enough of death for a while, and vowed to walk away from his beloved career, not having a clue as to what he'd do next, or where he'd end up. He'd live on his savings, and maybe open a pie shop somewhere. Gram used to make great pies. Her Key Lime pies were the best ever. Where he'd go, he had no idea. His plan was to get in his little car and head south. He had to feel the warmth of the sun on his face, maybe breathe in some salty air. He'd drive until he felt like stopping, and then drive some more after resting awhile, continuing the process until some new place felt right. Surely there would be a place where no one would look at him funny, or better yet, where no one would notice him at all. Maybe he'd adopt a cat along the way. Cats were nicer than people.

Sheriff Arlen Bemis cursed a blue streak when he entered the Cassel County jail and saw that the lone jailer had been murdered. The female officer was lying face down in a pool of blood, with a leaf-shaped patch of skin missing from her cheek. The sheriff had been assured that every precaution would be taken, but apparently the yokels running the tiny county jail had underestimated the ferocity of the bland-faced blonde woman, and now she was free. Bemis had a whole helluva lot of paperwork to do now, and was oddly relieved that when he went back to Pellman to warn Timothy Eckels that his psychotic wife had escaped, the mild-mannered mortician was already gone. Whether she'd catch up with her husband or not, wasn't Arlen's concern. There was a dangerous serial killer on the loose, and it was his fault. Retirement started looking awfully good all of the sudden.

Though he felt weird wearing shorts, when just days before he'd had a winter coat on, Timothy Eckels stripped off his shoes and socks, sinking his lily white feet into the sugary sands of a Key West beach, enjoying the warmth and texture on his toes. Making his way carefully down the beach, he sat down beneath a palm tree and contemplated the waves.

"Mew!" a plaintive sound from beside him caught his attention.

A tiny striped tabby sidled up and bonked her furry head against his thigh.

"Oh. Hello," the former mortician reached his hand out awkwardly, not wanting to scare the snuggly creature away. He scratched her between the ears and she nuzzled against his hand, purring.

Relationships with human beings were out of the question, but this non-judgmental little being seemed like she might be the perfect companion. The cat had no idea that he was weird, or introverted, or that one of his greatest joys was preparing the dead, nor did she care. He was warm and willing to pet her. It was all he had to give, and it was everything that she needed.

***

Captured by this foray into the psyche of a serial killer? Read more of Susannah's story in The Killing Girl, by Summer Prescott.

Made in the USA
Las Vegas, NV
28 April 2021